'Why are you waiting asked.

He had no answer.

'What do you want, Aaron?'

'I want you,' he said. Once it was out it seemed so easy. So clear. As though he *hadn't* spent agonising weeks telling himself she was the last thing he needed in his life. 'I haven't stopped wanting you. Not for a second.'

Her eyebrows arched upwards. Even her eyebrows were sexy.

'I think we've been through this already, haven't we?' she asked softly, and started to move past him.

His hand shot out. He saw it move, faster than his brain was working. Watched his fingers grip her upper arm.

She turned to face him.

He didn't know what he intended to do next—but at least she wasn't looking amused any more.

She looked hard at him for a moment. And then she took his face between her hands and kissed him, fusing her mouth to his with forceful passion. She pulled back a tiny fraction, then seemed to change her mind and kissed him again. Pulled back. Stepped back. Looked him in the eye.

'Now what?' she asked, her breathing unsteady.

That strange other being still had control of him. It was the only explanation for the way he jerked her close, crushed his arms around her and kissed her. 'Come upstairs,' he breathed against her mouth. 'Come with me.'

'All yours,' Ella said.

He grabbed her hand and walked quickly to the staircase, pulling her up it at a furious pace.

'Which way to your room?' he asked.

Silently, she guided him to it.

The room next to his.

Fate.

**Dear Reader**

As a diehard romantic, I like the idea of a love so strong it feels as if it's written in the stars. And that's a concept I've enjoyed exploring in FROM FLING TO FOREVER.

Aaron and Ella have known enough heartbreak to have them setting very specific life paths for themselves. But when they meet at a wedding in Australia those paths are destined for the scrapheap—they just don't know it yet.

It takes a second encounter—in Cambodia—to ignite a scorching but unwanted passion between them as they work side by side at a children's hospital.

And a third—in England—for them to realise that the passion isn't going away, so they'd better get it out of their systems with a quick, hard fling before sailing into their separate futures.

But it seems fate isn't so crazy about the 'fling' part.

I hope you enjoy the ride as Ella and Aaron face some tense situations and the occasional emergency as they re-set their life paths from fling to forever.

*Avril Tremayne*

# FROM FLING TO FOREVER

BY
AVRIL TREMAYNE

First published in Great Britain 2014
by Mills & Boon, an imprint of Harlequin (UK) Limited,
Large Print edition 2015
Eton House, 18-24 Paradise Road,
Richmond, Surrey, TW9 1SR

© 2014 Belinda de Rome

ISBN: 978-0-263-25471-6

Printed and bound in Great Britain
by CPI Antony Rowe, Chippenham, Wiltshire

**Avril Tremayne** read *Jane Eyre* as a teenager and has been hooked on tales of passion and romance ever since. An opportunistic insomniac, she has been a lifelong crazy-mad reader, but she took the scenic route to becoming a writer—via gigs as diverse as shoe salesgirl, hot-cross-bun-packer, teacher, and public relations executive. She has spent a good chunk of her life travelling, and has more favourite destinations than should be strictly allowable.

Avril is happily settled in her hometown of Sydney, Australia, where her husband and daughter try to keep her out of trouble—not always successfully. When she's not writing or reading she can generally be found eating—although she does *not* cook!

Check out her website: www.avriltremayne.com Or follow her on Twitter: @AvrilTremayne and Facebook: www.facebook.com/avril.tremayne

**FROM FLING TO FOREVER**
**is Avril Tremayne's debut book**
**for Mills & Boon® Medical Romance™!**

## Dedication

This book is dedicated to my fellow writer
PTG Man and Dr John Sammut with many,
many thanks for the generous medical advice.
Thanks also to Dr John Lander
and Dr Hynek Prochazka.
Any errors that snuck in
despite their best efforts are mine, all mine!

I would also like to acknowledge the amazing
Angkor Hospital for Children (AHC)—
a non-profit pediatric teaching hospital that
provides free quality care to impoverished
children in Siem Reap, Cambodia.
All the characters, settings and situations in
FROM FLING TO FOREVER are fictional—
however, during the course of my research,
I learned so much from AHC, which has
provided over one million medical treatments,
education to thousands of Cambodian health
workers, and prevention training to thousands
of families since it opened in 1999.
You can find out more about the hospital
at www.angkorhospital.org

# CHAPTER ONE

WEDDINGS.

Ella Reynolds had nothing against them, but she certainly didn't belong at one. Not even this one.

But her sister, Tina, had insisted she not only attend but trick herself out as maid of honour in this damned uncomfortable satin gown in which there was *no* stretch. Add in the ridiculous high heels and hair twisted into a silly bun that was pinned so tightly against her scalp she could practically feel the headache negotiating where to lunge first.

And then there was the stalker. Just to top everything off.

She'd first felt his stare boring into her as she'd glided up the aisle ahead of her sister. And then throughout the wedding service, when all eyes should have been on the bride and groom. And ever since she'd walked into the reception.

Disconcerting. And definitely unwanted.

Especially since he had a little boy with him. Gorgeous, sparkly, darling little boy. Asian. Three or four years old. Exactly the type of child to mess with her already messed-up head.

Ella looked into her empty champagne glass, debating whether to slide over the legal limit. Not that she was driving, but she was always so careful when she was with her family. Still…Tina, pregnant, glowing, deliriously happy, was on the dance floor with her new husband Brand—and not paying her any attention. Her parents were on the other side of the room, catching up with Brand's family on this rare visit to Sydney—and not paying her any attention. She was alone at the bridal table, with *no one* paying her any attention. Which was just fine with her. It was much easier to hold it all together when you were left to yourself. To not let anyone see the horrible, unworthy envy of Tina's pregnancy, Tina's *life*.

And—she swivelled around to look for a waiter—it made it much easier to snag that extra champagne.

But a sound put paid to the champagne quest. A cleared throat.

She twisted back in her chair. Looked up.

The stalker. *Uh-oh.*

'Hi,' he said.

'Hello.' Warily.

'So…you're Ella,' he said.

Oh, dear. *Inane* stalker. 'Yep. Sister of the bride.'

'Oh.' He looked surprised. And then, 'Sorry, the accent. I didn't realise…'

'I speak American, Tina speaks Australian. It does throw people. Comes of having a parent from each country and getting to choose where you live. I live in LA. Tina lives in Sydney. But it's still all English, you know.' Good Lord—*this* was conversation?

He laughed. 'I'm not sure the British see it that way.'

Okay—so now what? Ella wondered.

If he thought she was going to be charmed by him, he had another think coming. She *wasn't* going to be charmed. And she was *not* in the market for a pick-up tonight. Not that he wasn't attractive in a rough sort of way—the surfer-blond hair, golden tan and bursting muscles that looked completely out of place in a suit was a sexy combination. But she'd crossed the pick-up off her to-do list last night—and that had been a debacle, as usual. And even if she hadn't crossed it off the list, and it hadn't been a debacle, her sister's wedding was not the place for another attempt. Nowhere within a thousand *miles* of any of her relatives was the place.

'Do you mind if I sit and talk to you for a few minutes?' he asked, and smiled at her.

*Yes, I do.* 'Of course you can sit,' she said. Infinitesimal pause. 'And talk to me.'

'Great.' He pulled out a chair and sat. 'I think Brand warned you I wanted to pick your brains tonight.'

She frowned slightly. 'Brand?'

He smiled again. 'Um…your brother-in-law?'

'No-o-o, I don't think so.' Ella glanced over at Brand, who was carefully twirling her sister. 'I think he's had a few things on his mind. Marriage. Baby. Imminent move to London. New movie to make.'

Another smile. 'Right, let's start again and I'll introduce myself properly.'

Ella had to give the guy points for determination. Because he had to realise by now that if she really wanted to talk to him, she would have already tried to get his name out of him.

'I'm Aaron James,' he said.

Ella went blank for a moment, before the vague

memory surfaced. 'Oh. Of course. The actor. Tina emailed me about a…a film?' She frowned slightly. 'Sorry, I remember now. About malaria.'

'Yes. A documentary. About the global struggle to eradicate the disease. Something I am very passionate about, because my son… Well, too much information, I guess. Not that documentaries are my usual line of work.' Smile, but looking a little frayed. 'Maybe you've heard of a television show called *Triage*? It's a medical drama. I'm in that.'

'So…' She frowned again. 'Is it the documentary or the TV show you want to talk to me about? If it's the TV show, I don't think I can help you—my experience in city hospital emergency rooms is limited. And I'm a nurse—you don't look like you'd be playing a nurse. You're playing a doctor, right?'

'Yes, but—'

'I'm flying home tomorrow, but I know a few doctors here in Sydney and I'm sure they'd be happy to talk to you.'

'No, that's not—'

'The numbers are in my phone,' Ella said, reaching for her purse. 'Do you have a pen? Or can you—?'

Aaron reached out and put his hand over hers on the tiny bronze purse. 'Ella.'

Her fingers flexed, once, before she could stop them.

'It's not about the show,' he said, releasing her hand. 'It's the documentary. We're looking at treatments, mosquito control measures, drug resistance, and what's being done to develop a vaccine. We'll be shooting in Cambodia primarily—in some of the hospitals where I believe you've worked. We're not starting for a month, but I thought I should take the chance to talk to you while you're in Sydney. I'd love to get your impression of the place.'

She said nothing. Noted that he was starting to look impatient—and annoyed.

'Brand told me you worked for Frontline Medical Aid,' he prompted.

She controlled the hitch in her breath. 'Yes, I've worked for them, and other medical aid agencies, in various countries, including Cambodia. But I'm not working with any agency at the moment. And I'll be based in Los Angeles for the next year or so.'

'And what's it like? I mean, not Los Angeles— I know what— Um. I mean, the aid work.'

Ella shifted in her seat. He was just not getting it. 'It has its highs and lows. Like any job.'

He was trying that charming smile again. 'Stupid question?'

'Look, it's just a job,' she said shortly. 'I do what every nurse does. Look after people when they're sick or hurt. Try to educate them about health. That's all there is to it.'

'Come on—you're doing a little more than that. The conditions. The diseases that we just don't see here. The refugee camps. The landmines. Kidnappings, even.'

Her heart slammed against her ribs. Bang-bang-bang. She looked down at her hands, saw the whitened knuckles and dropped them to her lap, out of Aaron's sight. She struggled for a moment, getting herself under control. Then forced herself to look straight back up and right at him.

'Yes, the conditions are not what most medical personnel are used to,' she said matter-of-factly. 'I've seen the damage landmines can do. Had children with AIDS, with malnutrition, die in my arms. There have been kidnappings involving my colleagues, murders even. This is rare, but…' She stopped, raised an eyebrow. 'Is that the sort of detail you're looking for?' She forced herself to keep looking directly into his eyes. 'But I imagine you'll be insulated from the worst of it. They won't let anything happen to you.'

'I'm not worried about that,' Aaron said, with a quick shake of his head. Then, suddenly, he relaxed back in his chair. 'And you don't want to talk about it.'

*Eureka!* 'It's fine, really,' she said, but her voice dripped with insincerity.

The little boy Ella had seen earlier exploded onto the scene, throwing himself against Aaron's leg, before the conversation could proceed.

'Dad, look what Tina gave me.'

*Dad.* So, did he have an Asian wife? Or was the little boy adopted?

Aaron bent close to smell the small rose being offered to him.

'It's from her bunch of flowers,' the little boy said, blinking adorably.

'Beautiful.' Aaron turned laughing eyes to Ella. 'Ella, let me introduce my son, Kiri. Kiri, this is Tina's sister, Ella.'

Kiri. He was Cambodian, then. And he'd had malaria—that was Aaron's TMI moment. 'Nice to meet you Kiri,' Ella said, with a broad smile, then picked up her purse. 'Speaking of Tina and flowers, it must be time to throw the bouquet. I'd better go.'

She got to her feet. 'Goodbye Aaron. Good luck with the documentary. Goodbye Kiri.'

Well, that had been uncomfortable, Ella thought as she left the table, forcing herself to walk slowly. Calm, controlled, measured—the way she'd trained herself to walk in moments of stress.

Clearly, she had to start reading her sister's emails more carefully. She recalled, too late, that Tina's email had said Aaron was divorced; that he had an adopted son—although not that the boy was Cambodian, because *that* she would have remembered. She'd made a reference to the documentary. And there probably had been a mention of talking to him as a favour to Brand, although she really couldn't swear to it.

She just hadn't put all the pieces together and equated them with the wedding, or she would have been better prepared for the confrontation.

*Confrontation*. Since when did a few innocent questions constitute a confrontation?

Ella couldn't stop a little squirm of shame. Aaron wasn't to know that the exact thing he wanted to talk about was the exact thing she couldn't bring herself to discuss with anyone. Nobody knew about Sann, the beautiful little Cambodian boy who'd died of malaria before she'd even been able to start the adoption process. Nobody knew about her relationship with Javier—her colleague and lover, kidnapped in Somalia and still missing. Nobody knew because she hadn't *wanted* anyone to know, or to worry about her. Hadn't wanted anyone to push her to talk about things, relive what she couldn't bear to relive.

So, no, Aaron wasn't to be blamed for asking what he thought were standard questions.

But he'd clearly sensed something was wrong with her. Because he'd gone from admiration— oh, yes, she could read admiration—to something akin to dislike, in almost record time. Something in those almost sleepy, silver-grey eyes had told her she just wasn't his kind of person.

Ella's head had started to throb. The damned pins.

Ah, well, one bouquet-toss and last group hug with her family and she could disappear. Back to her hotel. Throw down some aspirin. And raid the mini-bar, given she never had got that extra glass of champagne.

*Yeah, like raiding the mini-bar has ever helped*, her subconscious chimed in.

'Oh, shut up,' she muttered.

Well, that had been uncomfortable, Aaron thought as Ella Reynolds all but bolted from the table. Actually, she'd been walking slowly. Too slowly. Unnaturally slowly.

Or maybe he was just cross because of ego-dent. Because one woman in the room had no idea who he was. And didn't *care* who he was when she'd found out. Well, she was American—why *would* she know him? He wasn't a star over there.

Which wasn't the point anyway.

Because since when did he expect people to recognise him and drool?

Never!

But celebrity aside, to be looked at with such blank disinterest…it wasn't a look he was used to from women. Ella Reynolds hadn't been over-whelmed. Or deliberately *under*whelmed, as sometimes happened. She was just…hmm, was 'whelmed' a word? Whelmed. Depressing.

*Ego, Aaron—so* not *like you.*

Aaron swallowed a sigh as the guests started

positioning themselves for the great bouquet toss. Ella was in the thick of it, smiling. Not looking in his direction—on purpose, or he'd eat the roses.

She was as beautiful as Tina had said. More so. Staggeringly so. With her honey-gold hair that even the uptight bun couldn't take the gloss off. The luminous, gold-toned skin. Smooth, wide forehead. Finely arched dusky gold eyebrows and wide-spaced purple-blue eyes with ridiculously thick dark lashes. Lush, wide, pouty mouth. No visible freckles. No blemishes. The body beneath the figure- hugging bronze satin she'd been poured into for the wedding was a miracle of perfect curves. Fabulous breasts—and silicone-free, if he were any judge. Which he was, after so many years in the business.

And the icing on the cake—the scent of her. Dark and musky and delicious.

Yep. Stunner.

But Tina had said that as well as being gorgeous her sister was the best role model for women she could think of. Smart, dedicated to her work, committed to helping those less fortunate regardless of the personal danger she put herself in regularly.

Well, sorry, but on the basis of their conversation tonight he begged to differ. Ella Reynolds was no role model. There was something wrong with her. Something that seemed almost...dead. Her smile—that dazzling, white smile—didn't reach her eyes. Her eyes had been beautifully *empty*. It had been almost painful to sit near her.

Aaron felt a shiver snake down his spine.

On the bright side, he didn't feel that hot surge of desire—that bolt that had hit him square in the groin the moment she'd slid into the church—any more. Which was good. He didn't want to lust after her. He didn't have the time or energy or emotional availability to lust after anyone.

He turned to his beautiful son. 'Come on, Kiri—this part is fun to watch. But leave the bouquet-catching to the girls, huh?'

*We're not going down that road again, bouquet or not*, he added silently to himself.

## CHAPTER TWO

ELLA HAD BEEN determined to spend a full year in Los Angeles.

But within a few weeks of touching down at LAX she'd been back at the airport and heading for Cambodia. There had been an outbreak of dengue fever, and someone had asked her to think about helping out, and she'd thought, *Why not?*

Because she just hadn't been feeling it at home. Whatever 'it' was. She hadn't felt right since Tina's wedding. Sort of restless and on edge. So she figured she needed more distraction. More work. More…something.

*And volunteering at a children's hospital in mosquito heaven is just the sort of masochism that's right up your alley, isn't it, Ella?*

So, here she was, on her least favourite day of the year—her birthday—in northwest Cambodia—and because it *was* her birthday she was in the bar of one of the best hotels in town instead of her usual cheap dive.

Her parents had called this morning to wish her happy birthday. Their present was an airfare to London and an order to use it the moment her time in Cambodia was up. It was framed in part as a favour to Tina: stay with her pregnant sister in her new home city and look after her health while Brand concentrated on the movie. But she knew Tina would have been given her own set of orders: get Ella to rest and for goodness' sake fatten her up—because her mother always freaked when she saw how thin and bedraggled Ella was after a stint in the developing world.

Tina's present to Ella was a goat. Or rather a goat in Ella's name, to be given to an impoverished community in India. Not every just-turned-twenty-seven-year-old's cup of tea, but so totally perfect for this one.

And in with the goat certificate had been a parcel with a note: 'Humour me and wear this.' 'This' was sinfully expensive French lingerie in gorgeous mint-green silk, which Ella could never have afforded. It felt like a crime wearing it under her flea-market gypsy skirt and bargain-basement singlet top. But it did kind of cheer her up. Maybe she'd have to develop an underwear fetish—although somehow she didn't think she'd find this kind of stuff digging around in the discount bins the way she usually shopped.

A small group of doctors and nurses had dragged her out tonight. They'd knocked back a few drinks, told tales about their life experiences and then eventually—inevitably—drifted off, one by one, intent on getting some rest ahead of another busy day.

But Ella wasn't due at the hospital until the afternoon, so she could sleep in. Which meant she could stay out. And she had met someone—as she always seemed to do in bars. So she'd waved the last of her friends off with a cheerful guarantee that she could look after herself.

Yes, she had met someone. Someone who might help make her feel alive for an hour or two. Keep the nightmares at bay, if she could bring herself to get past the come-on stage for once and end up in bed with him.

She felt a hand on her backside as she leaned across the pool table and took her shot. She missed the ball completely but looked back and smiled. Tom. British. Expat. An...engineer, maybe?

*Was* he an engineer? Well, who cared? Really, who cared?

He pulled her against him, her back against his chest. Arms circled her waist. Squeezed.

She laughed as he nipped at her earlobe, even though she couldn't quite stop a slight shudder of distaste. His breath was too hot, too...moist. He bit gently at her ear again.

Ella wasn't sure what made her look over at the entrance to the bar at that particular moment. But pool cue in one hand, caught against Tom's chest, with—she realised in one awful moment—one of the straps of her top hanging off her shoulder to reveal the beacon-green silk of her bra strap, she looked.

Aaron James.

He was standing still, looking immaculately clean in blue jeans and a tight white T-shirt, which suited him way more than the get-up he'd been wearing at the wedding. Very tough-guy gorgeous, with the impressive muscles and fallen-angel hair with those tousled, surfer-white streaks she remembered very well.

Actually, she was surprised she remembered so much!

He gave her one long, cool, head-to-toe inspection. One nod.

Ah, so he obviously remembered her too. She was pretty sure that was not a good thing.

Then he walked to the bar, ignoring her. *Hmm.* Definitely *not a good thing.*

Ella, who'd thought she'd given up blushing, blushed. Hastily she yanked the misbehaving strap back onto her shoulder.

With a wicked laugh, Tom the engineer nudged it back off.

'Don't,' she said, automatically reaching for it again.

Tom shrugged good-humouredly. 'Sorry. Didn't mean anything by it.'

For good measure, Ella pulled on the long-sleeved, light cotton cardigan she'd worn between her guesthouse accommodation and the hotel. She always dressed for modesty outside Western establishments, and that meant covering up.

And there were mosquitoes to ward off in any case.

And okay, yes, the sight of Aaron James had unnerved her. She admitted it! She was wearing a cardigan because Aaron James had looked at her in *that* way.

She tried to appear normal as the game pro-gressed, but every now and then she would catch Aaron's gaze on her and she found it increas-ingly difficult to concentrate on the game or on Tom. Whenever she laughed, or when Tom let out a whoop of triumph at a well-played shot, she would feel Aaron looking at her. Just for a moment. His eyes on her, then off. When Tom went to the bar to buy a round. When she tripped over a chair, reaching for her drink. When Tom enveloped her from behind to give her help she didn't need with a shot.

It made her feel…dirty. Ashamed. Which was just not fair. She was single, adult, independent. So she wanted a few mindless hours of fun on her lonely birthday to take her mind off sickness and death—what was wrong with that?

But however she justified things to herself, she knew that tonight her plans had been derailed. All because of a pair of censorious silver eyes.

Censorious eyes that belonged to a friend of her sister. Very sobering, that—the last thing she needed was Aaron tattling to Tina about her.

It was probably just as well to abandon to-night's escapade. Her head was starting to ache and she felt overly hot. Maybe she was coming down with something? She would be better off in bed. Her bed. Alone. As usual.

She put down her cue and smiled at Tom the engineer. Her head was pounding now. 'It's been fun, Tom, but I'm going to have to call it a night.'

'But it's still early. I thought we could—'

'No, really. It's time I went home. I'm tired, and I'm not feeling well.'

'Just one more drink,' Tom slurred, reaching for her arm.

She stepped back, out of his reach. 'I don't think so.'

Tom lunged for her and managed to get his arms around her.

He was very drunk, but Ella wasn't concerned. She'd been in these situations before and had always managed to extricate herself. Gently but firmly she started to prise Tom's arms from around her. He took this as an invitation to kiss her and landed his very wet lips on one side of her mouth.

*Yeuch.*

Tom murmured something about how beautiful she was. Ella, still working at unhooking his arms, was in the middle of thanking him for the compliment when he suddenly wasn't there. One moment she'd been disengaging herself from his enthusiastic embrace, and the next—air.

And then an Australian accent. 'You don't want to do that, mate.'

She blinked, focused, and saw that Aaron James was holding Tom in an embrace of his own, standing behind him with one arm around Tom's chest. How had he got from the bar to the pool table in a nanosecond?

'I'm fine,' Ella said. 'You can let him go.'

Aaron ignored her.

'I said I'm fine,' Ella insisted. 'I was handling it.'

'Yes, I could see that,' Aaron said darkly.

'I was,' Ella insisted, and stepped forward to pull futilely at Aaron's steel-band arm clamped across Tom's writhing torso.

Tom lunged at the same time, and Ella felt a crack across her lip. She tasted blood, staggered backwards, fell against the table and ended up on the floor.

And then everything swirled. Black spots. Nothing.

The first thing Ella noticed as her consciousness returned was the scent. Delicious. Clean and wild, like the beach in winter. She inhaled. Nuzzled her nose into it. Inhaled again. She wanted to taste it. Did it taste as good as it smelled? She opened her mouth, moved her lips, tongue. One small lick. Mmm. Good. Different from the smell but…good.

Then a sound. A sharp intake of breath.

She opened her eyes. Saw skin. Tanned skin. White next to it. She shook her head to clear it. Oh, that hurt. Pulled back a little, looked up. Aaron James. 'Oh,' she said. 'What happened?'

'That moron knocked you out.'

It came back at once. Tom. 'Not on purpose.'

'No, not on purpose.'

'Where is he?'

'Gone. Don't worry about him.'

'I'm not worried. He's a big boy. He can take care of himself.' Ella moved again, and realised she was half lolling against Aaron's thighs.

She started to ease away from him but he kept her there, one arm around her back, one crossing her waist to hold onto her from the front.

'Take it easy,' Aaron said.

A crowd of people had gathered around them. Ella felt herself blush for the second time that night. Intolerable, but apparently uncontrollable. 'I don't feel well,' she said.

'I'm not surprised,' Aaron replied.

'I have to get home,' she said, but she stayed exactly where she was. She closed her eyes. The smell of him. It was him, that smell. That was… comforting. She didn't know why that was so. Didn't care why. It just was.

'All right, people, show's over,' Aaron said, and Ella realised he was telling their audience to get lost. He said something more specific to another man, who seemed to be in charge. She assumed he was pacifying the manager. She didn't care. She just wanted to close her eyes.

'Ella, your lip's bleeding. I'm staying here at the hotel. Come to my room, let me make sure you're all right, then I'll get you home. Or to the hospital.'

She opened her eyes. 'Not the hospital.' She didn't want anyone at the hospital to see her like this.

'Okay—then my room.'

She wanted to say she would find her *own* way home *immediately*, but when she opened her mouth the words 'All right' were what came out. She ran her tongue experimentally over her lip. *Ouch*. Why hadn't she noticed it was hurting? 'My head hurts more than my lip. Did I hit it when I fell?'

'No, I caught you. Let me…' He didn't bother finishing the sentence, instead running his fingers over her scalp. 'No, nothing. Come on. I'll help you stand.'

Aaron carefully eased Ella up. 'Lean on me,' he said softly, and Ella didn't need to be told twice. She felt awful.

As they made their way out of the bar, she noted a few people looking and whispering, but nobody she knew. 'I'm sorry about this,' she said to Aaron. 'Do you think anyone knows you? I mean, from the television show?'

'I'm not well known outside Australia. But it doesn't matter either way.'

'I don't want to embarrass you.'

'I'm not easily embarrassed. I've got stories that would curl your hair. It's inevitable, with three semi-wild younger sisters.'

'I was all right, you know,' she said. 'I can look after myself.'

'Can you?'

'Yes. I've been doing it a long time. And he was harmless. Tom.'

'Was he?'

'Yes. I could have managed. I *was* managing.'

'Were you?'

'Yes. And stop questioning me. It's annoying. And it's hurting my head.'

They were outside the bar now and Aaron stopped. 'Just one more,' he said, and turned her to face him. 'What on earth were you thinking?'

Ella was so stunned at the leashed fury in his voice she *couldn't* think, let alone speak.

He didn't seem to need an answer, though, because he just rolled right on. 'Drinking like a fish. Letting that clown slobber all over you!'

'He's not a clown, he's an engineer,' Ella said. And then, with the ghost of a smile, 'And fish don't drink beer.'

He looked like thunder.

Ella waited, curious about what he was going to hurl at her. But with a snort of disgust he simply took her arm again, started walking.

He didn't speak again until they were almost across the hotel lobby. 'I'm sorry. I guess I feel a little responsible for you, given my relationship with Brand and Tina.'

'That is just ridiculous—I already have a father. And he happens to know I can look after myself.

Anyway, why are you here?' Then, 'Oh, yeah, I remember. The documentary.' She grimaced. '*Should* I have known you'd be here now?'

'I have no idea. Anyway, you're supposed to be in LA.'

'I was in LA. But now— It was a sudden decision, to come here. So it looks like we've surprised each other.'

'Looks like it.'

Aaron guided Ella through a side door leading to the open air, and then along a tree-bordered path until they were in front of what looked like a miniature mansion. He *would* be in one of the presidential-style villas, of course. He didn't look very happy to have brought her there, though.

'How long will you be in town?' she asked, as he unlocked the door.

'Two weeks, give or take.'

'So, you'll be gone in two weeks. And I'll still be here, looking after myself. Like I've always done.' She was pleased with the matter-of-factness of her voice, because in reality she didn't feel matter-of-fact. She felt depressed. She blamed it on the birthday.

Birthdays: misery, with candles.

'Well, good for you, Ella,' he said, and there

was a definite sneer in there. 'You're doing such a fine job of it my conscience will be crystal clear when I leave.'

*Hello? Sarcasm? Really? Why?*

Aaron drew her inside, through a tiled hallway and into a small living room. There was a light on but no sign of anyone.

'Is your son with you?' she asked. *Not that it's any of your business, Ella.*

'Yes, he's in bed.'

'So you've got a nanny? Or is your wife—?' *Um, not your business?*

'Ex-wife. Rebecca is in Sydney. And, yes, I have a nanny, whose name is Jenny. I don't make a habit of leaving my four-year-old son on his own in hotel rooms.'

Oh, dear, he really did *not* like her. And she was well on the way to actively disliking *him*. His attitude was a cross between grouchy father and irritated brother—without the familial affection that would only just make that bearable.

Aaron gestured for Ella to sit. 'Do you want something to drink?'

Ella sank onto the couch. 'Water, please.'

'Good choice,' Aaron said, making Ella wish she'd asked for whisky instead.

He went to the fridge, fished out a bottle of water, poured it into a glass and handed it to her. She didn't deign to thank him.

She rubbed her forehead as she drank.

He was watching her. 'Head still hurting?'

'Yes.'

'Had enough water?'

Ella nodded and Aaron took the glass out of her hand, sat next to her. He turned her so she was facing away from him. 'Here,' he said tetchily, and started kneading the back of her neck.

'Ahhh…' she breathed out. 'That feels good.'

'Like most actors, I've had a chequered career—massage therapy was one of my shorter-lived occupations but I remember a little,' Aaron said, sounding not at all soothing like a massage therapist.

'Where's the dolphin music?' she joked.

He didn't bother answering and she decided she would *not* speak again. She didn't see why she should make an effort to talk to him, given his snotty attitude. She swayed a little, and he pulled her closer to his chest, one hand kneading while he reached his other arm around in front of her, bracing his forearm against her collarbone to balance her.

She could smell him again. He smelled exqui-site. So clean and fresh and…yum. The rhythmic movement of his fingers was soothing, even if it did nothing to ease the ache at the front of her skull. She could have stayed like that for hours.

Slowly, he finished the massage and she had to bite back a protest. He turned her to face him and looked at her lip. 'It's only a small tear. I have a first-aid kit in the bathroom.'

'How very *Triage* of you, Aaron.' He looked suitably unimpressed at that dig.

'Just some ice,' she said. 'That's all I need. And I can look after it myself. I'm a nurse, remem-ber?'

But Aaron was already up and away.

He came back with a bowl of ice and the first-aid kit.

Ella peered into the kit and removed a square of gauze, then wrapped it around an ice cube. 'It's not serious and will heal quickly. Mouth injuries do. It's all about the blood supply.'

Not that Aaron seemed interested in that piece of medical information, because he just took the wrapped ice from her impatiently.

'I promise you I can do it myself,' Ella said.

'Hold still,' he insisted. He held the ice on her bottom lip, kept it pressed there for a minute.

'Open,' he ordered, and Ella automatically opened her mouth for him to inspect inside. 'Looks like you bit the inside of your lip.' He grabbed another square of gauze, wrapped it around another cube of ice and pressed it on the small wound.

He was looking intently at her mouth and Ella started to feel uncomfortable. She could still smell that heavenly scent wafting up from his skin. Why couldn't he smell like stale sweat like everyone else in that bar? She blinked a few times, trying to clear her fuzzy head.

Her eyes fell on his T-shirt and she saw a smear of blood on the collar. Her blood. Her fingers reached out, touched it. His neck, too, had a tiny speck of her blood. Seemingly of their own volition her fingers travelled up, rubbing at the stain. And then she remembered how it had got there. Remembered in one clear flash how she had put her mouth there, on his skin. She felt a flare of arousal and sucked in a quick breath.

He had gone very still. He was watching her. Looking stunned.

# CHAPTER THREE

'SORRY,' ELLA SAID. 'It's just… I—I bled on you.'

'Ella, I don't think it's a good idea for you to touch me.'

'Sorry,' Ella said again, jerking her fingers away.

Aaron promptly contradicted himself by taking the hand she'd pulled away and pressing it against his chest. He could actually *hear* his heart thudding. It was probably thumping against her palm like a drum. He didn't care. He wanted her hand on him. Wanted both her hands on him.

He could hear a clock ticking somewhere in the room, but except for that and his heart the silence was thick and heavy.

*I don't even like her.* He said that in his head, but something wasn't connecting his head to his groin, because just as the thought completed itself he tossed the gauze aside and reached for her other hand, brought it to his mouth, pressed his mouth there, kept it there.

Okay, so maybe you didn't have to like some-one to want them.

He really, really hadn't expected to see her again. She was supposed to be in LA. Their 'relationship' should have begun and ended with one awkward conversation at a wedding.

And yet here he was. And here she was. And he had no idea what was going to happen next.

When he'd walked into that bar tonight and seen her with that idiot, he'd wanted to explode, drag her away, beat the guy senseless.

And he *never* lost his temper!

He'd been so shocked at his reaction he'd con-templated leaving the bar, going somewhere else—a different bar, for a walk, to bed, any-thing, anywhere else. But he hadn't.

He'd only been planning on having one drink anyway, just a post-flight beer. But nope. He'd stayed, sensing there was going to be trouble. She'd laughed too much, drunk too much, Tom the idiot engineer had fondled her too much. Something was going to give.

And something definitely had.

And of course he'd been there smack bang in the middle of it, like he couldn't get there fast enough.

And then his arms had been around her. And she'd snuggled against him. Her tongue on his neck. And he'd wanted her. Wanted her like he'd never wanted anyone in his life.

And it had made him furious.

Was making him furious now.

So why was he moving the hand he'd been holding to his mouth down to his chest, instead of letting it go?

His hands were only lightly covering hers now. She could break away if she wanted to. Bring him back to sanity. *Please.*

But she didn't break away.

Her hands moved up, over his chest to his collarbones then shoulders. Confident hands. Direct and sure.

He stifled a groan.

'You don't want me.' She breathed the words. 'You don't like me.' But her hands moved again, down to his deltoids, stopping there. Her fingers slid under the short sleeves of his T-shirt, stroked.

This time the groan escaped as his pulse leapt.

Ella moved closer to him, sighed as she surrounded him with her arms, rested the side of her face against his chest then simply waited.

He battled himself for a long moment. His hand

hovered over her hair. He could see the tremor in his fingers. He closed his eyes so the sight of her wouldn't push him over the edge. That only intensified the sexy smell of her. Ella Reynolds. Tina's *sister*. 'I can't,' he said. 'I can't do this.' Was that his voice? That croak?

He waited, every nerve tingling. Didn't trust himself to move. If he moved, even a fraction...

Then he heard her sigh again; this time it signalled resignation, not surrender.

'No, of course not,' she said, and slowly disentangled herself until she was sitting safely, separately, beside him.

*Whew. Catastrophe averted.*

'A shame,' she said. Her voice was cool and so were her eyes as she reached out to skim her fingernail over his right arm, at the top of his biceps where the sleeve of his T-shirt had been pushed up just enough to reveal the lower edge of a black tattoo circlet. Her lips turned up in an approximation of a smile. 'Because I like tattoos. They're a real turn-on for me. Would have been fun.'

He stared at her, fighting the urge to drag her back against his chest, not quite believing the disdainful humour he could hear in her voice, see in her eyes. Wondering if he'd imagined the yielding softness only moments ago.

At Tina and Brand's wedding he'd sensed that there was something wrong with her. It had made him uncomfortable to be near her. Made him want to get away from her.

He had the same feeling now. Only this time he couldn't get away. He would be damned if he'd let Tina's sister stagger home drunk and disorderly, with a pounding head and a split lip. *Oh, yeah, that's the reason, is it? Tina?*

Ella shrugged—a dismissive, almost delicate gesture. 'But don't worry, I won't press you,' she said calmly. 'I've never had to beg for it in my life and I won't start now, tattoos or not.'

She stood suddenly and smiled—the dazzling smile that didn't reach her eyes. 'I'd better go,' she said.

'I'll take you home,' he said, ignoring the taunt of all those men she hadn't had to beg. None of his business.

'I'll walk.'

'I'll take you,' Aaron insisted.

Ella laughed. 'Okay, but I hope we're not going to drag some poor driver out of bed.'

'Where are you staying?'

'Close enough. I can walk there in under ten minutes.'

'Then we'll walk.'

'All right, then, lead on, Sir Galahad,' Ella said lightly, mockingly.

And that was *exactly* why he didn't like her.

Because she was just so unknowable. Contrary. Changeable. Ready to seduce him one moment and the next so cool. Poised. Amused. They made it to the street without him throttling her, which was one relief. Although he would have preferred a different relief—one for inside his jeans, because, heaven help him, it was painful down there. How the hell did she *do* that? Make him both want her and want to run a mile in the opposite direction?

Ella led off and Aaron fell into step beside her, conscious of her excruciatingly arousing perfume. The almost drugging combination of that scent, the damp heat, the sizzle and shout of the street stalls, the thumping music and wild shouts from the tourist bars, was so mesmerisingly exotic it felt almost like he was in another world. One where the normal rules, the checks and balances, didn't apply.

The minutes ticked by. A steady stream of motorbikes puttered past. A short line of tuk-tuks carrying chatty tourists. Jaunty music from a group of street musicians. Sounds fading as he and Ella walked further, further.

'Needless to say, tonight's escapade is not something Tina needs to hear about,' Ella said suddenly.

'Needless to say,' he agreed.

A tinkling laugh. 'Of course, you wouldn't want it getting back to your wife either. At least, not the latter part of the evening.'

'Ex-wife,' Aaron corrected her. He heard a dog barking in the distance. A mysterious rustle in the bushes near the road.

'Ah.' Ella's steps slowed, but only very briefly. 'But not really ex, I'm thinking, Sir Galahad.'

Aaron grabbed Ella's arm, pulling her to the side of a dirty puddle she was about to step into. 'It's complicated,' he said, when she looked at him.

She pulled free of the contact and started forward again.

'But definitely ex,' he added. And if she only knew the drug-fuelled hell Rebecca had put him through for the past three years, she would understand.

'Oh, dear, how inconvenient! An ex who's not really an ex. It must play havoc with your sex life.'

She laughed again, and his temper got the better of him.

The temper that he *never* lost.

'What is wrong with you?' he demanded, whirling her to face him.

She looked up at him, opened her mouth to say—

Well, who knew? Because before he could stop himself he'd slapped his mouth on hers in a devouring kiss.

Just what he *didn't* want to do.

And she had the audacity to kiss him back. More than that—her arms were around him, her hands under his T-shirt.

Then he tasted blood, remembered her lip. Horrified, he pulled back. 'I'm sorry,' he said.

She ran her tongue across her lower lip, raised her eyebrows. '*Definitely* would have been fun,' she said.

'I'm not looking for a relationship,' he said bluntly. And where had that come from? It seemed to suggest he *was* after *something*. But what? What was he after? Nothing—nothing from her.

It seemed to startle her, at least. 'Did I ask for one?'

'No.'

'That's a relief! Because I'm really only interested in casual sex. And on that note, how fortunate that we're here. Where I live. So we can say our goodbyes, and both pretend tonight didn't happen. No relationship. And, alas, no casual sex, because you're married. Oh, no, that's right, you're not. But no sex anyway.'

'I should have left you with the engineer.'

'Well, I would have seen a lot more action,' she said. She started forward and then stopped, raised her hand to her eyes.

'What is it?' Aaron asked.

'Nothing. A headache,' she answered. 'I'll be fine.'

'Goodbye, then,' he said, and turned to walk back to the hotel.

*A lot more action!* Ha! Aaron was quite sure if he ever let himself put his hands on Ella Reynolds she wouldn't be able to think about another man for a long time. Or walk straight either.

But he was not going to touch her, of course. *Not*.

Ella made her way to her room, cursing silently.

Her head was throbbing and her joints were aching and she longed to lapse into a thought-free coma. She'd just realised she'd contracted either malaria or dengue fever. She wasn't sure which, but either way it sucked.

But when she'd taken two paracetamol tablets and clambered into bed, praying for a mild dose of whatever it was, it wasn't the pain that made the tears come. It was shame. And regret. And a strange sense of loss.

Aaron James had wanted her. Ordinarily, a man wanting her would not cause Ella consternation. Lots of men had wanted her and she'd had no trouble resisting them.

But Aaron was different. He'd kissed her like he was pouring his strength, his soul into her. And yet he'd been able to fight whatever urge had been driving him.

Why? How?

She manhandled her pillow, trying to get it into a more head-cradling shape.

Not looking for a relationship—that's what he'd said. How galling! As though it were something she would be begging for on the basis of one kiss. All right, one *amazing* kiss, but—seriously! What a joke. A relationship? The one thing she *couldn't* have.

Ella sighed as her outrage morphed into something more distressing: self-loathing. Because she was a fraud and she knew it. A coward who used whatever was at her disposal to stop herself from confronting the wreck her life had become since Javier had been kidnapped in Somalia on her twenty-fifth birthday.

She'd been in limbo ever since. Feeling helpless, hopeless. Guilty that she was free and he was who-knew-where. In the year after his kidnapping she'd felt so lost and alone and powerless she'd thought a nervous breakdown had been on the cards.

And then she'd found Sann in a Cambodian orphanage, and life had beckoned to her again. Two years old, and hers. Or so she'd hoped. But he'd been taken too. He'd died, on her twenty-sixth birthday.

And now here she was on her twenty-*seventh* birthday. Still in limbo, with no idea of what had happened to Javier. Still grieving for Sann.

Panicking at the thought of seeing an Asian child with an adoptive parent.

Unable to entertain even the thought of a relationship with a man.

Pretending she was calm and in control when she was a basket case.

Her life had become a series of shambolic episodes. Too many drinks at the bar. Getting picked up by strange men, determined to see it through then backing out. *Always* backing out, like the worst kind of tease, because no matter how desperate she was to feel *something*, the guilt was always stronger. Coping, but only just, with endlessly sad thoughts during the day and debilitating dreams at night.

She knew that something in her was lost— but she just didn't know how to find it. She hid it from the people she cared about because she knew her grief would devastate them. She hid it from her colleagues because they didn't need the extra burden.

And she was just…stuck. Stuck on past heartbreaks. And it was starting to show.

No wonder Aaron James abhorred the idea of a 'relationship' with her.

Ella rubbed tiredly at her forehead. She closed her eyes, longing for sleep, but knowing the nightmares would come tonight.

Dr Seng slapped his hand on the desk and Aaron's wandering mind snapped back to him. 'So— we've talked about malaria. Now, a few facts about the hospital.'

Kiri had been whisked off to do some painting—one of his favourite pastimes—on arrival at the Children's Community Friendship Hospital, so Aaron could concentrate on this first meeting.

But he wasn't finding it easy.

He had a feeling… A picture of Ella here. Was this where she was working? He wasn't sure, but he kept expecting her to sashay past.

Dr Seng handed over an array of brochures. 'Pre-Pol Pot, there were more than five hundred doctors practising in Cambodia,' Dr Seng said. 'By the time the Khmer Rouge fled Cambodia in 1979 there were less than fifty. Can you imagine what it must have been like? Rebuilding an entire healthcare system from the ground up, with almost no money, no skills? Because that's what happened in Cambodia.'

Aaron knew the history—he'd made it his business to know, because of Kiri. But he could never come to terms with the brutal stupidity of the Khmer Rouge. 'No, I can't imagine it,' he said simply. 'And I'd say this hospital is something of a miracle.'

'Yes. We were started by philanthropists and we're kept going by donations—which is why we are so happy to be associated with your documentary: we need all the publicity we can get, to keep attracting money. It costs us less than twenty-five dollars to treat a child. Only fifty dollars to operate. Unheard of in your world. But, of course, we have so many to help.'

'But your patients pay nothing, right?'

'Correct. Our patients are from impoverished communities and are treated free, although they contribute if they can.'

'And your staff...?'

'In the early days the hospital relied on staff from overseas, but today we are almost exclusively Khmer. And we're a teaching hospital—we train healthcare workers from all over the country. That's a huge success story.'

'So you don't have any overseas staff here at the moment?'

'Actually, we do. Not paid staff—volunteers.'

'Doctors?'

'We have a group of doctors from Singapore coming in a few months' time to perform heart surgeries. And at the moment we have three nurses, all from America, helping out.'

'I was wondering if…' Aaron cleared his throat. 'If perhaps Ella Reynolds was working here?'

Dr Seng looked at him in surprise. 'Ella? Why, yes!'

*Ahhhhh.* Fate. It had a lot to answer for.

'I—I'm a friend. Of the family,' Aaron explained.

'Then I'm sorry to say you probably won't see her. She's not well. She won't be in for the whole week.'

Aaron knew he should be feeling relieved. He could have a nice easy week of filming, with no cutting comments, no tattoo come-ons, no amused eyebrow-raising.

But…what did 'not well' mean? Head cold? Sprained toe? Cancer? Liver failure? Amputation? 'Not well?'

'Dengue fever—we're in the middle of an outbreak, I'm afraid. Maybe a subject for your next documentary, given it's endemic in at least a hundred countries and infects up to a hundred million people a year.'

Alarm bells. 'But it doesn't kill you, right?'

'It certainly can,' the doctor said, too easily, clearly not understanding Aaron's need for reassurance.

Aaron swallowed. 'But…Ella…'

'Ella? No, no, no. She isn't going to die. The faster you're diagnosed and treated the better, and she diagnosed herself very quickly. It's more dangerous for children, which Ella is not. And much more dangerous if you've had it before, which Ella has not.'

Better. But not quite good enough. 'So is she in hospital?'

'Not necessary at this stage. There's no cure; you just have to nurse the symptoms—take painkillers, keep up the fluids, watch for signs of internal bleeding, which would mean it was dengue haemorrhagic fever—very serious! But Ella knows what she's doing, and she has a friend staying close by, one of the nurses. And I'll be monitoring her as well. A shame it hit her on her birthday.'

'Birthday?'

'Two days ago. Do you want me to get a message to her?'

'No, that's fine,' Aaron said hurriedly. 'Maybe I'll see her before I head home to Sydney.'

'Then let's collect Kiri and I'll have you both taken on a tour of our facilities.'

It quickly became clear that it was Kiri, not Aaron, who was the celebrity in the hospital. He seemed to fascinate people with his Cambodian Australian-ness, and he was equally fascinated in return. He got the hang of the *satu*—the graceful greeting where you placed your palms together and bowed your head—and looked utterly natural doing it. It soothed Aaron's conscience, which had been uneasy about bringing him.

They were taken to observe the frenetic outpatient department, which Aaron was stunned to learn saw more than five hundred patients a day in a kind of triage arrangement.

The low acuity unit, where he saw his first malaria patients, a sardine can's worth of dengue sufferers, and children with assorted other conditions, including TB, pneumonia, malnutrition, HIV/AIDS and meningitis.

The emergency room, where premature babies and critically ill children were treated for sepsis, severe asthma, and on and on and on.

Then the air-conditioned intensive care unit, which offered mechanical ventilation, blood gas analysis and inotropes—not that Aaron had a clue what that meant. It looked like the Starship *Enterprise* in contrast to the mats laid out for the overflow of dengue sufferers in the fan-cooled hospital corridors.

The tour wrapped up with a walk through the basic but well-used teaching rooms, some of which had been turned into makeshift wards to cope with the dengue rush.

And then, to Aaron's intense annoyance, his focus snapped straight back to Ella.

Tina and Brand would expect him to check on her, right?

And, okay, *he* wanted to make sure for himself that she was going to recover as quickly and easily as Dr Seng seemed to think.

One visit to ease his conscience, and he would put Ella Reynolds into his mental lockbox of almost-mistakes and double-padlock the thing.

And so, forty minutes after leaving the hospital, with Kiri safely in Jenny's care at the hotel, he found himself outside Ella's guesthouse, coercing her room number from one of the other boarders, and treading up the stairs.

# CHAPTER FOUR

AARON FELT SUDDENLY guilty as he knocked. Ella would have to drag herself out of bed to open the door.

Well, why not add another layer of guilt to go with his jumble of feelings about that night at the bar?

The boorish way he'd behaved—when he was *never* boorish.

The way he'd assumed her headache was the result of booze, when she'd actually been coming down with dengue fever.

The door opened abruptly. A pretty brunette, wearing a nurse's uniform, stood there.

'Sorry, I thought this was Ella Reynolds's room,' Aaron said.

'It is.' She gave him the appreciative look he was used to receiving from women—women who weren't Ella Reynolds, anyway. 'She's in bed. Ill.'

'Yes, I know. I'm Aaron James. A…a friend. Of the family.'

'I'm Helen. I'm in the room next door, so I'm keeping an eye on her.'

'Nice to meet you.'

She gave him a curious look and he smiled at her, hoping he looked harmless.

'Hang on, and I'll check if she's up to a visit,' Helen said.

The door closed in his face, and he was left wondering whether it would open again.

What on earth was he doing here?

Within a minute Helen was back. 'She's just giving herself a tourniquet test, but come in. I'm heading to the hospital, so she's all yours.'

It was gloomy in the room. And quiet—which was why he could hear his heart racing, even though his heart had no business racing.

His eyes went first to the bed—small, with a mosquito net hanging from a hook in the ceiling, which had been shoved aside. Ella was very focused, staring at her arm, ignoring him. So Aaron looked around the room. Bedside table with a lamp, a framed photo. White walls. Small wardrobe. Suitcase against a wall. A door that he guessed opened to a bathroom, probably the size of a shoebox.

He heard a sound at the bed. Like a magnet, it drew him.

She was taking a blood-pressure cuff off her arm.

'I heard you were ill,' he said, as he reached the bedside. 'I'm sorry. That you're sick, I mean.'

'I'm not too happy about it myself.' She sounded both grim and amused, and Aaron had to admire the way she achieved that.

'Who told you I was sick?' she asked.

'The hospital. I'm filming there for the next week.'

She looked appalled at that news. 'Just one week, right?'

'Looks like it.'

She nodded. He imagined she was calculating the odds of having to see him at work. Flattering—not.

He cleared his throat. 'So what's a tourniquet test?'

'You use the blood-pressure machine—'

'Sphygmomanometer.'

'Well, aren't you clever, Dr *Triage*! Yes. Take your BP, keep the cuff blown up to halfway between the diastolic and systolic—the minimum and maximum pressure—wait a few minutes and check for petechiae—blood points in the skin.'

'And do you have them? Um…it? Petechiae?'

'Not enough. Less than ten per square inch.'

'Is that…is that bad?'

'It's good, actually.'

'Why?'

Audible sigh. 'It means I have classic dengue—not haemorrhagic. As good as it gets when every bone and joint in your body is aching and your head feels like it might explode through your eyeballs.'

'Is that how it feels?'

'Yes.'

Silence.

Aaron racked his brain. 'I thought you might want me to get a message to Tina.'

Her lips tightened. Which he took as a no.

'That would be no,' she confirmed.

A sheet covered the lower half of her body. She was wearing a red T-shirt. Her hair was piled on top of her head, held in place by a rubber band. Her face was flushed, a light sheen of sweat covering it. And despite the distinct lack of glamour, despite the tightened lips and warning eyes, she was the most beautiful woman he'd ever seen.

'Shouldn't you keep the net closed?' he asked, standing rigid beside the bed. Yep—just the sort of thing a man asked a nurse who specialised in tropical illnesses.

'Happy to, if you want to talk to me through it. Or you can swat the mosquitoes before they get to me.'

'Okay—I'll swat.'

She regarded him suspiciously. 'Why are you really here? To warn me I'll be seeing you at the hospital?'

'No, because it looks like you won't be. I just wanted to make sure you were all right. See if you needed anything.'

'Well, I'm all right, and I don't need anything. So thank you for coming but...' Her strength seemed to desert her then and she rolled flat onto her back in the bed, staring at the ceiling, saying nothing.

'I heard it was your birthday. That night.'

An eye roll, but otherwise no answer.

He came a half-step closer. 'If I'd known...'

Aaron mentally winced as she rolled her eyes again.

'What would you have done?' she asked. 'Baked me a cake?'

'Point taken.'

Trawling for a new topic of conversation, he picked up the photo from her bedside table. 'Funny—you and Tina sound nothing alike, and you look nothing alike.'

Silence, and then, grudgingly, 'I take after my father's side of the family. Tina's a genetic throwback.' She smiled suddenly, and Aaron felt his breath jam in his throat. She really was gorgeous when she smiled like that, with her eyes as well as her mouth—even if it was aimed into space and not at him.

He gestured to the photo. 'I wouldn't have picked you for a Disneyland kind of girl.'

'Who doesn't like Disneyland? As long as you remember it's not real, it's a blast.'

Aaron looked at her, disturbed by the harshness in her voice. Did she have to practise that cynicism or did it come naturally?

Ella raised herself on her elbow again. 'Look, forget Disneyland, and my birthday. I *do* need something from you. Only one thing.' She fixed him with a gimlet eye. 'Silence. You can't talk about that night, or about me being sick. Don't tell Tina. Don't tell Brand. My life here has nothing to do with them. In fact, don't talk to anyone about me.'

'Someone should know you've got dengue fever.'

'*You* know. That will have to do. But don't worry, it won't affect you unless I don't make it. And my advice then would be to head for the hills and forget you were ever in Cambodia, because my mother will probably kill you.' That glorious smile again—and, again, not directed at him, just at the thought. 'She never did like a bearer of bad tidings—quite medieval.'

'All the more reason to tell them now.'

Back to the eye roll. 'Except she's not really going to kill you and I'm not going to drop dead. Look...' Ella seemed to be finding the right words. 'They'll worry, and I don't want them worrying about something that can't be changed.'

'You shouldn't be on your own when you're ill.'

'I'm not. I'm surrounded by experts. I feel like I'm in an episode of your TV show, there are so many medical personnel traipsing in and out of this room.'

Aaron looked down at her.

'Don't look at me like that,' Ella said.

'Like what?' Aaron asked. But he was wincing

internally because he kind of knew how he must be looking at her. And it was really inappropriate, given her state of health.

With an effort, she pushed herself back into a sitting position. 'Let me make this easy for you, Aaron. I am not, ever, going to have sex with you.'

Yep, she'd pegged the look all right.

'You have a child,' she continued. 'And a wife, ex-wife, whatever. And it's very clear that your… encumbrances…are important to you. And that's the way it *should* be. I understand it. I respect it. I even admire it. So let's just leave it. I was interested for one night, and now I'm not. You were interested, but not enough. Moment officially over. You can take a nice clear conscience home to Sydney, along with the film.'

'Ella—'

'I don't want to hear any more. And I really, truly, do not want to see you again. I don't want— Look, I don't want to get mixed up with a friend of my sister's. Especially a man with a kid.'

Okay, sentiments Aaron agreed with wholeheartedly. So he should just leave it at that. Run— don't walk—to the nearest exit. Good riddance. So he was kind of surprised to find his mouth opening and 'What's Kiri got to do with it?' coming out of it.

'It's just a…a thing with children. I get attached to them, and it can be painful when the inevitable goodbyes come around—there, something about me you didn't need to know.'

'But you're working at a children's hospital.'

'That's my business. But the bottom line is—I don't want to see Kiri. Ergo, I don't want to see you.' She stopped and her breath hitched painfully. 'Now, please…' Her voice had risen in tone and volume and she stopped. As he watched, she seemed to gather her emotions together. 'Please go,' she continued quietly. 'I'm sick and I'm tired and I— Just please go. All right?'

'All right. Message received loud and clear. Sex officially off the agenda. And have a nice life.'

'Thank you,' she said, and tugged the mosquito net closed.

Aaron left the room, closed the door and stood there.

Duty discharged. He was free to go. *Happy* to go.

But there was some weird dynamic at work, because he couldn't seem to make his feet move.

His overgrown sense of responsibility, he told himself.

He'd taken two steps when he heard the sob. Just one, as though it had been cut off. He could picture her holding her hands against her mouth to stop herself from making any tell-tale sound. He hovered, waiting.

But there was only silence.

Aaron waited another long moment.

There was something about her. Something that made him wonder if she was really as prickly as she seemed…

He shook his head. No, he wasn't going to wonder about Ella Reynolds. He'd done the decent thing and checked on her.

He was not interested in her further than that. Not. Interested.

He forced himself to walk away.

Ella had only been away from the hospital for eight lousy days.

How did one mortal male cause such a disturbance in so short a time? she wondered as she batted away what felt like the millionth question about Aaron James. The doctors and nurses, male and female, Khmer and the small sprinkling of Westerners, were uniformly goggle-eyed over him.

*Knock yourselves out*, would have been Ella's attitude; except that while she'd been laid low by the dengue, Aaron had let it slip to Helen—and therefore everyone!—that he was a close friend of Ella's film director brother-in-law. Which part of 'Don't talk to anyone about me' didn't he understand?

As a result, the whole, intrigued hospital expected her to be breathless with anticipation to learn what Aaron said, what Aaron did, where Aaron went. They expected Ella to marvel at the way he dropped in, no airs or graces, to talk to the staff; how he spoke to patients and their families with real interest and compassion, even when the cameras weren't rolling; the way he was always laughing at himself for getting ahead of his long-suffering translator.

He'd taken someone's temperature. Whoop-de-doo!

And had volunteered as a guinea pig when they'd been demonstrating the use of the rapid diagnostic test for malaria—yeah, so one tiny pinprick on his finger made him a hero?

And had cooked alongside a Cambodian father

in the specially built facility attached to the hospital. Yee-ha!

And, and, and, *and*—give her a break.

All Ella wanted to do was work, without hear-
ing his name. They'd had their moment, and it
had passed. Thankfully he'd got the message and
left her in peace once she'd laid out the situation.
She allowed herself a quick stretch before moving onto the next child—a two-year-old darling
named Maly. *Heart rate. Respiration rate. Blood
pressure. Urine output. Adjust the drip.*

The small hospital was crowded now that the
dengue fever outbreak was peaking. They were
admitting twenty additional children a day, and
she was run off her still-wobbly legs. In the midst
of everything she should have been too busy to
sense she was being watched…and yet she knew.

She turned. And saw him. Aaron's son, Kiri,
beside him.

Wasn't the hospital filming supposed to be
over? Why was he here?

'Ella,' Aaron said. No surprise. Just acknowl-
edgement.

She ignored the slight flush she could feel
creeping up from her throat. With a swallowed
sigh she fixed on a smile and walked over to him.

She would be cool. Professional. Civilised. She held out her hand. 'Hello, Aaron.'

He took it, but released it quickly.

'And *sua s'day*, Kiri,' she said, crouching in front of him. 'Do you know what that means?'

Kiri shook his head. Blinked.

'It means hello in Khmer. Do you remember me?'

Kiri nodded. '*Sua s'day*, Ella. Can I go and see her?' he asked, looking over, wide-eyed, at the little girl Ella had been with.

'Yes, you can. But she's not feeling very well. Do you think you can be careful and quiet?'

Kiri nodded solemnly and Ella gave him a confirming nod before standing again. She watched him walk over to Maly's bed before turning to reassure Aaron. 'She's not contagious. It's dengue fever and there's never been a case of person-to-person transmission.'

'Dr Seng said it deserved its own documentary. The symptoms can be like malaria, right? But it's a virus, not a parasite, and the mosquitoes aren't the same.'

Ella nodded. 'The dengue mosquito—' She broke off. 'You're really interested?'

'Why wouldn't I be?'

'I just...' She shrugged. 'Nothing. People can get bored with the medical lingo.'

'I won't be bored. So—the mosquitoes?'

'They're called *Aedes aegypti*, and they bite during the day. Malaria mosquitoes—*Anopheles*, but I'm sure you know that—get you at night, and I'm sure you know that too. It kind of sucks that the people here don't get a break! Anyway, *Aedes aegypti* like urban areas, and they breed in stagnant water—vases, old tyres, buckets, that kind of thing. If a mosquito bites someone with dengue, the virus will replicate inside it, and then the mosquito can transmit the virus to other people when it bites them.' Her gaze sharpened. 'You're taking precautions for Kiri, aren't you?'

'Oh, yes. It's been beaten it into me. Long sleeves, long pants. Insect repellent with DEET. And so on and so forth.'

'You too—long sleeves, I mean. Enough already with the T-shirts.'

'Yes, I know. I'm tempting fate.'

Silence.

He was looking at her in that weird way.

'So, the filming,' she said, uncomfortable. 'Is it going well?'

'We're behind schedule, but I don't mind because it's given me a chance to take Kiri to see Angkor Wat. And the place with the riverbed carvings. You know, the carvings of the genitalia.' He stopped suddenly. 'I—I mean, the… um…Hindu gods…you know…and the—the… ah…Kal…? Kab…?'

Ella bit the inside of her cheek. It surprised her that she could think he was cute. But he sort of was, in his sudden embarrassment over the word genitalia. 'Yes, I know all about genitalia. And it's Kbal Spean, you're talking about, and the Hindu God is Shiva. It's also called The River of a Thousand Lingas—which means a thousand stylised phalluses,' she said, and had to bite her cheek again as he ran a harassed hand into his hair.

'So, the filming?' she reminded him.

'Oh. Yeah. A few more days here and then the final bit involves visiting some of the villages near the Thai border and seeing how the malaria outreach programme works, with the volunteers screening, diagnosing and treating people in their communities.'

'I was out there a few years ago,' Ella said. 'Volunteers were acting as human mosquito bait. The mosquitoes would bite them, and the guys would scoop them into test tubes to be sent down to the lab in Phnom Penh for testing.'

'But wasn't that dangerous? I mean…*trying* to get bitten?'

'Well, certainly drastic. But all the volunteers were given a combination drug cocktail, which meant they didn't actually develop malaria.'

'So what was the point?'

'To verify whether the rapid treatment malaria programme that had been established there was managing to break the pathways of transmission between insects, parasites and humans. But you don't need to worry. That was then, this is now. And they won't be asking you to roll up your jeans and grab a test tube.'

'Would you have rolled up your jeans, Ella?'

'Yes.'

'And risked malaria?'

'I've had it. Twice, actually. Once in Somalia, once here.'

'Somalia?'

*Uh-oh. She was not going there.* 'Obviously, it didn't kill me, either time. But I've *seen* it kill. It kills one child every thirty seconds.' She could hear her voice tremble so she paused for a moment. When she could trust herself, she added, 'And I would do anything to help stop that.'

Aaron was frowning. Watching her. Making her feel uncomfortable. Again. 'But you're not— Sorry, it's none of my business, but Kiri isn't going with you up there, right?'

'No.' Aaron frowned. Opened his mouth. Closed it. Opened. Closed.

'Problem?' she prompted.

'No. But... Just...' Sigh.

'Just...?' she prompted again.

'Just—do you think I made a mistake, bringing him to Cambodia?' he asked. 'There were reasons I couldn't leave him at home. And I thought it would be good for him to stay connected to his birth country. But, like you, he's had malaria. Before the adoption.'

'Yes, I gathered that.'

'I'd never forgive myself if he got it again because I brought him with me.'

Ella blinked at him. She was surprised he would share that fear with her—they weren't exactly friends, after all—and felt a sudden emotional connection that was as undeniable as it was unsettling.

She wanted to touch him. Just his hand. She

folded her arms so she couldn't. 'I agree that children adopted from overseas should connect with their heritage,' she said, ultra-professional. And then she couldn't help herself. She unfolded her arms, touched his shoulder. Very briefly. 'But, yes, we're a long way from Sydney, and the health risks are real.'

'So I shouldn't have brought him?'

'You said there were reasons for not leaving him behind—so how can I answer that? But, you know, these are diseases of poverty we're talking about. That's a horrible thing to acknowledge, but at least it can be a comfort to you. Because you know your son would have immediate attention, the *best* attention—and therefore the best outcome.'

He sighed. 'Yes, I see what you mean. It is horrible, and also comforting.'

'And it won't be long until you're back home. Meanwhile, keep taking those precautions, and if he exhibits any symptoms, at least you know what they are—just don't wait to get him to the hospital.'

She swayed slightly, and Aaron reached out to steady her.

'Sorry. Tired,' she said.

'You're still not fully recovered, are you?' he asked.

'I'm fine. And my shift has finished so I'm off home in a moment.'

Ella nodded in Kiri's direction. The little boy was gently stroking the back of Maly's hand. 'He's sweet.'

'Yes. He's an angel.'

'You're lucky,' Ella said. She heard the…thing in her voice. The wistfulness. She blinked hard. Cleared her throat. 'Excuse me, I need to— Excuse me.'

Ella felt Aaron's eyes on her as she left the ward.

Ella was doing that too-slow walk. Very controlled.

She'd lost her curves since the wedding. She'd been thin when he'd visited her a week ago, but after the dengue she was like a whippet.

But still almost painfully beautiful. Despite the messy ponytail. And the sexless pants and top combo that constituted her uniform.

And he still wanted her.

He'd been furious at how he'd strained for a sight of her every time he'd been at the hospital, even though he'd known she was out of action. Seriously, how pathetic could a man be?

He'd tried and tried to get her out of his head. No joy. There was just something…something under the prickly exterior.

Like the way she looked at Kiri when he'd repeated her Cambodian greeting. The expression on her face when she'd spoken about diseases of the poor. It was just so hard to reconcile all the pieces. To figure out that *something* about her.

He caught himself. Blocked the thought. Reminded himself that if there *was* something there, he didn't want it. One more week, and he would never have to see or think of her again. He could have his peace of mind back. His libido back under control.

He called Kiri over and they left the ward.

And she was there—up the corridor, crouching beside a little boy who was on one of the mattresses on the floor, her slender fingers on the pulse point of his wrist.

*Arrrgggghhh*. This was *torture*. Why wasn't she on her way home like she was supposed to be, so he didn't have to see her smile into that little boy's eyes? Didn't have to see her sit back on her heels and close her eyes, exhausted?

And wonder just who she really was, this woman who was prickly and dismissive. Knowledgeable and professional. Who wouldn't think twice about letting mosquitoes bite her legs for research. Who looked at sick children with a tenderness that caused his chest to ache. Who made him feel gauche and insignificant.

Who made him suddenly and horribly aware of what it was like to crave something. Someone. It was so much more, so much *worse*, than purely physical need.

'Ow,' Kiri protested, and Aaron loosened his hold on Kiri's hand.

Ella looked up, saw them. Froze. Nodding briefly, she got to her feet and did that slow walk out.

This was not good, Aaron thought.

A few days and he would be out of her life.

Ella felt that if only she didn't have to converse with Aaron again, she would cope with those days.

But she hadn't banked on the *sight* of him being such a distraction. Sauntering around like a doctor on regular rounds, poking his nose in everywhere without even the excuse of a camera. Not really coming near her, but always *there*.

It was somehow worse that he was keeping his distance, because it meant there was no purpose to the way she was perpetually waiting for him to show up.

Him and the boy, who reminded her so much of Sann.

It was painful to see Kiri, even from a distance. So painful she shouldn't want to see him, shouldn't want the ache it caused. Except that alongside the pain was this drenching, drowning need. She didn't bother asking why, accepting that it was a connection she couldn't explain, the way it had been with Sann.

On her fourth day back at work, after broken sleep full of wrenching nightmares, the last thing she needed was Aaron James, trailed by his cameraman, coming into the outpatient department just as a comatose, convulsing two-year-old boy was rushed up to her by his mother.

The look in Ella's eyes as she reached for the child must have been terrible because Aaron actually ran at her. He plucked the boy from his mother's arms. 'Come,' he said, and hurried through the hospital as though he'd worked there all his life, Ella and the little boy's mother hurrying after him.

This was a child. Maybe with malaria. And Aaron was helping her.

How was she supposed to keep her distance now?

# CHAPTER FIVE

AARON SIGNALLED FOR the cameraman to start filming as what looked like a swarm of medical people converged on the tiny little boy in the ICU.

Ella was rattling off details as he was positioned in the bed—name Bourey, two years old, brought in by his mother after suffering intermittent fever and chills for two days. Unable to eat. Seizure on the way to the hospital. Unable to be roused. Severe pallor. Second seizure followed.

Hands, stethoscopes were all over the boy—pulling open his eyelids, taking his temperature. Checking heart rate, pulse and blood pressure. *Rash? No.* Feeling his abdomen.

*I want a blood glucose now.*

Into Bourey's tiny arm went a canula.

Blood was taken, and whisked away.

*Intravenous diazepam as a slow bolus to control the seizures.*

The doctor was listening intently to Bourey's

breathing, which was deep and slow. The next moment the boy was intubated and hooked up to a respirator.

Every instruction was rapid-fire.

'Intravenous paracetamol for the fever.'

'Intravenous artesunate, stat, we won't wait for the blood films—we'll treat for falciparum malaria. Don't think it's menigococcus but let's give IV benzylpenicillin. We'll hold off on the lumbar puncture. I want no evidence of focal neuro signs. What was his glucose?'

'Intravenous dextrose five per cent and normal saline point nine per cent for the dehydration—but monitor his urine output carefully; we don't want to overdo it and end up with pulmonary oedema, and we need to check renal function. And watch for haemoglobinuria. If the urine is dark we'll need to cross-match.'

Overhead an assortment of bags; tubes drip, drip, dripping.

How much stuff could the little guy's veins take?

A urinary catheter was added to Bourey's overloaded body. Empty plastic bag draped over the side of the bed.

A plastic tube was measured, from the boy's

nose to his ear to his chest, lubricated, threaded up Bourey's nose, taped in place.

'Aspirate the stomach contents.'

'Monitor temp, respiratory rate, pulse, blood pressure, neuro obs every fifteen minutes.'

*Hypoglycaemia, metabolic acidosis, pulmonary oedema, hypotensive shock. Watch the signs. Monitor. Check. Observe.*

Aaron's head was spinning. His cameraman silent and focused as he filmed.

And Ella—so calm, except for her eyes.

Aaron was willing her to look at him. And every time she did, she seemed to relax. Just a slight breath, a softening in her face so subtle he could be imagining it, a lessening of tension in her shoulders. Then her focus was back to the boy.

The manic pace around Bourey finally eased and Aaron saw Ella slip out of the ICU. Aaron signalled to his cameraman to stop filming and left the room.

They had enough to tell the story but they needed a face on camera.

He went in search of Dr Seng, wanting to check the sensitivity of the case and get suggestions for the best interviewee.

Dr Seng listened, nodded, contemplated. Undertook to talk to Bourey's family to ascertain their willingness to have the case featured. 'For the interview, I recommend Ella,' he said. 'She knows enough about malaria to write a textbook, and she is highly articulate.'

Aaron suspected the ultra-private Ella would rather eat a plate of tarantulas and was on the verge of suggesting perhaps a doctor when Ella walked past.

Dr Seng beckoned her over, asked for her participation and smiled genially at them before hurrying away.

Ella looked at Aaron coolly. 'Happy to help, of course,' she said.

They found a spot where they were out of the way of traffic but with a view through the ICU windows. The cameraman opted for handheld, to give a sense of intimacy.

*Great—intimacy.*

'Well?' she asked, clearly anxious to get it done.

'Don't you want to…?' He waved a hand at his hair. At his face.

'What's wrong with the way I look?'

'Nothing. It's just that most people—'

'What's more important, how my hair looks or that little boy?'

'Fine,' Aaron said. 'Tell me about the case.'

'This is a two-year-old child, suffering from cerebral falciparum malaria. Blood films showed parasitaemia—'

'Parasitaemia?'

'It means the number of parasites in his blood. His level is twenty-two per cent. That is high and very serious. Hence the IV artesunate—a particular drug we use for this strain—which we'll administer for twenty-four hours. After that, we'll switch to oral artemisinin-based combination therapy—ACT for short. It's the current drug regime for falciparum. We'll be monitoring his parasitaemia, and we'd expect to see the levels drop relatively quickly.'

She sounded smart and competent and in control.

'And if they don't drop?' Aaron asked.

Her forehead creased. 'Then we've got a problem. It will indicate drug resistance. This region is the first in the world to show signs of resistance to ACTs, which used to kill the parasites in forty-eight hours and now take up to ninety-six hours. It was the same for previous treatments like

cloroquine, which is now practically useless—
we're like the epicentre for drug resistance here.'

'How does it happen, the resistance?'

'People take just enough of the course to feel better. Or the medicines they buy over the counter are substandard, or counterfeit, with only a tiny fraction of the effective drug in it. Or they are sold only a fraction of the course. Often the writing on the packet is in a different language, so people don't know what they're selling, or buying. And here we have highly mobile workers crossing the borders—in and out of Thailand, for example. So resistant strains are carried in and out with them. The problem is there's no new miracle drug on the horizon, so if we don't address the resistance issue...' She held out her hands, shrugged. Perfection for the camera. 'Trouble. And if the resistance eventually gets exported to Africa—as history suggests it will—it will be catastrophic. Around three thousand children die of malaria every day in sub-Saharan Africa, which is why this is a critical issue.'

He waited. Letting the camera stay on her face, letting the statistic sink in. 'Back to this particular case. What happens now?'

'Continuous clinical observation and measuring what's happening with his blood, his electrolytes. I could give you a range of medical jargon but basically this is a critically ill child. We hope his organs won't fail. We hope he doesn't suffer any lifelong mental disabilities from the pressure on his brain. But, first, we hope he survives.'

A forlorn hope, as it turned out.

One minute they had been working to save Bourey's life, preparing for a whole-blood transfusion to lower the concentration of parasites in Bourey's blood and treat his anaemia. The next, Ella was unhooking him from the medical paraphernalia that had defined his last hours.

She left the ICU and her eyes started to sting. She stopped, wiped a finger under one eye, looked down at it. Wet. She was crying. And what was left of the numbness—one year's worth of carefully manufactured numbness—simply fell away.

She heard something and looked up. She saw Aaron, and tried to pull herself together. But her body had started to shake, and she simply had no reserves of strength left to pretend everything was all right.

A sobbing sort of gasp escaped her, a millisecond before she could put her hand over her mouth to stop it. Her brain and her heart and her body seemed to be out of synch. Her limbs couldn't seem to do what she was urging them to do. So the horrible gasp was followed by a stumble as she tried to turn away. She didn't want Aaron to see her like this. Didn't want anybody to see her, but especially not Aaron. He knew her sister. He might tell her sister. Her sister couldn't know that she was utterly, utterly desolate.

'I'm fine,' she said, as she felt his hand on her shoulder, steadying her.

Aaron withdrew his hand. 'You don't look fine,' he said.

Ella shook her head, unable to speak. She took one unsteady step. Two. Stopped. The unreleased sobs were aching in her chest. Crushing and awful. She had to get out of the hospital.

She felt Aaron's hand on her shoulder again and found she couldn't move. Just couldn't force her feet in the direction she wanted to go.

Aaron put his arm around her, guiding her with quick, purposeful strides out of the hospital, into the suffocating heat, steering her towards and then behind a clump of thick foliage so they were out of sight.

Ella opened her mouth to tell him, again, that she was fine, but… 'I'm sorry,' she gasped instead. 'I can't— Like Sann. My Sann. Help me, help me.'

He pulled her into his arms and held on. 'I will. I will, Ella. Tell me how. Just tell me.'

'He died. He died. I c-c-couldn't stop it.'

Aaron hugged her close. Silence. He seemed to know there was nothing to say.

Ella didn't know how long she stood there, in Aaron James's arms, as the tears gradually slowed. It was comforting, to be held like this. No words. Just touch. She didn't move, even when the crying stopped.

Until he turned her face up to his. And there was something in his eyes, something serious and concerned.

A look that reminded her Aaron James could not be a shoulder to cry on. He was too…close, somehow. She didn't want anyone to be close to her. Couldn't risk it.

Ella wrenched herself out of his arms. Gave a small, self-conscious hunch of one shoulder. 'It shouldn't upset me any more, I know. But sometimes…' She shoved a lank lock of hair behind her ear. 'Usually you think if they had just got to us faster…they are so poor, you see, that they wait, and hope, and maybe try other things. Because it is expensive for them, the trip to the hospital, even though the treatment is free. But in this case I think…I think nothing would have made any difference… And I…I hate it when I can't make a difference.'

She rubbed her tired hands over her face. 'Usually when I feel like this I donate blood. It reminds me that things that cost me nothing can help someone. And because the hospital always needs so much blood. But I can't even do that now because it's too soon after the dengue. So I've got nothing. Useless.'

'I'll donate blood for you,' Aaron said immediately.

She tried to smile. 'You're doing something important already—the documentary. And I didn't mind doing that interview, you know. I'd do anything.'

She started to move away, but he put his hand on her arm, stopping her.

'So, Ella. Who's Sann?'

Ella felt her eyes start to fill again. Through sheer will power she stopped the tears from spilling out. He touched her, very gently, his hand on her hair, her cheek, and it melted something. 'He was the child I wanted to adopt,' she said. And somehow it was a relief to share this. 'Here in Cambodia. A patient, an orphan, two years old. I went home to find out what I had to do, and while I was gone he…he died. Malaria.'

'And you blame yourself,' he said softly. 'Because you weren't there. Because you couldn't save him. And I suppose you're working with children in Cambodia, which must torture you, as a kind of penance.'

'I don't know.' She covered her face in her hands for one long moment. Shuddered out a breath. 'Sorry—it's not something I talk about.' Her hands dropped and she looked at him, drained of all emotion. 'I'm asking you not to mention it to Tina. She never knew about Sann. And there's no point telling her. She doesn't need to know about this episode today either. Can I trust you not to say anything?'

'You can trust me. But, Ella, you're making a mistake. This is not the way to—'

'Thank you,' she said abruptly, not wanting to hear advice she couldn't bear to take. 'The rain… it's that time of the day. And I can feel it coming. Smell it.'

'So? What's new?'

'I'd better get back.'

'Wait,' he called.

But Ella was running for the hospital.

She reached the roof overhang as the heavens opened. Looked back at Aaron, who hadn't moved, hadn't taken even one step towards shelter. He didn't seem to care that the gushing water was plastering his clothes to his skin.

He was watching her with an intensity that scared her.

Ella shivered in the damp heat and then forced her eyes away.

The next day Helen told Ella that Aaron James had been in and donated blood.

For her. He'd done it for her.

But she looked at Helen as though she couldn't care less. The following day, when Helen reported that Aaron had left for his visit to the villages, same deal. But she was relieved.

She hoped Aaron would be so busy that any thought of her little breakdown would be wiped out of his mind.

Meanwhile, she would be trying to forget the way Aaron had looked at her—like he understood her, like he knew how broken she was. Trying to forget *him*.

There was only one problem with that: Kiri.

Because Kiri and Aaron came as a set.

And Ella couldn't stop thinking, worrying, about Kiri. Knowing that the cause was her distress over Bourey's death didn't change the fact that she had a sense of dread about Kiri's health that seemed tied to Aaron's absence.

Which just went to prove she was unhinged!

*Kiri has a nanny to look after him. It's none of your business, Ella.*

She repeated this mantra to herself over and over.

But the nagging fear kept tap-tapping at her nerves as she willed the time to pass quickly until Aaron could whisk his son home to safety.

When she heard Helen calling her name frantically two days after Aaron had left, her heart started jackhammering.

'What?' Ella asked, hurrying towards Helen. But she knew. *Knew.*

'It's Aaron James. Or rather his son. He's been taken to the Khmer International Hospital. Abdominal pains. Persistent fever. Retro-orbital pain. Vomiting. They suspect dengue fever.'

Ella felt the rush in her veins, the panic.

'They can't get hold of Aaron,' Helen said. 'So the nanny asked them to call us because she knows he's been filming here. I thought you should know straight away, because— Well, the family connection. Ella, what if something goes wrong and we can't reach Aaron?'

Ella didn't bother to answer. She simply ran.

Aaron had been unsettled during his time in the monsoonal rainforest.

Not that it hadn't been intriguing—the medical challenges the people faced.

And confronting—the history of the area, which had been a Khmer Rouge stronghold, with regular sightings of people with missing limbs, courtesy of landmines, to prove it.

And humbling—that people so poor, so constantly ill, should face life with such stoic grace.

And beautiful, even with the daily downpours—with the lush, virgin forest moist enough to suck at you, and vegetation so thick you had the feeling that if you stood still for half an hour, vines would start growing over you, anchoring you to the boggy earth.

But!

His mobile phone was bothering him. He'd never been out of contact with Kiri before, but since day two, when they'd headed for the most remote villages that were nothing more than smatterings of bamboo huts on rickety stilts, he'd had trouble with his phone.

He found himself wishing he'd told Jenny to contact Ella if anything went wrong. But Jenny, not being psychic, would never guess that was what Aaron would want her to do—not when she'd never heard Ella's name come out of his mouth. Because he'd been so stupidly determined *not* to talk about Ella, in a misguided attempt to banish her from his head. And what an epic fail *that* had been, because she was still in his head. Worse than ever.

He'd hoped being away from the hospital would cure it.

Not looking likely, though.

Every time he saw someone with a blown-off limb, or watched a health worker touch a malnourished child or check an HIV patient, he remembered Ella's words at the wedding reception. *I've seen the damage landmines can do. Had children with AIDS, with malnutrition, die in my arms.* He hadn't understood how she could sound so prosaic but now, seeing the endless stream of injuries, illness, poverty, he did.

And anything to do with malaria—well, how could he not think of her, and that searing grief?

The malaria screening process in the villages was simple, effective. Each person was registered in a book. *Ella, in the outpatient department, recording patient details.*

They were checked for symptoms—simple things like temperature, spleen enlargement. *Ella's hands touching children on the ward.*

Symptomatic people went on to the rapid diagnostic test. Fingertip wiped, dried. Squeeze the finger gently, jab quickly with a lancet. Wipe the first drop, collect another drop with a pipette. Drop it into the tiny well on the test strip. Add buffer in the designated spot. Wait fifteen minutes for the stripes to appear. *Ella, soothing children as their blood was siphoned off at the hospital.*

Aaron helped distribute insecticide-impregnated mosquito nets—a wonderfully simple method of protecting against malaria and given out free. *Ella, blocking him out so easily just by tugging her bed net closed.*

*Arrrggghhh.*

But relief was almost at hand. One last interview for the documentary and he would be heading back to Kiri. Jenny would have already packed for the trip home to Sydney. Ella would be out of his sight, out of his reach, out of his life once they left Cambodia.

Just one interview to go.

He listened closely as the village volunteer's comments were translated into English. There were three thousand volunteers throughout Cambodia, covering every village more than five kilometres from a health centre, with people's homes doubling as pop-up clinics. Medication was given free, and would be swallowed in front of the volunteers to make sure the entire course was taken. People diagnosed with malaria would not only have blood tested on day one but also on day three to assess the effectiveness of the drug treatment. *Ella, explaining drug resistance. Mentioning so casually that she'd had malaria twice.*

Half an hour later, with the filming wrapped up, they were in the jeep.

Twenty minutes after that his phone beeped. Beeped, beeped, beeped. Beeped.

He listened with the phone tight to one ear, fingers jammed in the other to block other sounds.

Felt the cold sweat of terror.

If he hadn't been sitting, his legs would have collapsed beneath him.

Kiri. Dengue haemorrhagic fever. His small, gentle, loving son was in pain and he wasn't there to look after him.

His fault. All his. He'd brought Kiri to Cambodia in the middle of an outbreak. Left him while he'd traipsed off to film in the boondocks, thinking that was the safer option.

He listened to the messages again. One after the other. Progress reports from the hospital—calm, matter-of-fact, professional, reassuring. Jenny—at first panicked, tearful. And then calmer each time, reassured by one of the nurses. Rebecca frantic but then, somehow, also calmer, mentioning an excellent nurse.

Three times he'd started to call the Children's Community Friendship Hospital to talk to Ella, wanting her advice, her reassurance, her skills to be focused on Kiri. Three times he'd stopped himself—he *had* expert advice, from Kiri's doctor and a tropical diseases specialist in Sydney he'd called.

And Ella had made it clear she wanted nothing to do with him.

And his son wasn't Ella's problem. Couldn't be her problem.

He wouldn't, couldn't let her mean that much.

The hospital where Kiri had been taken was like a five-star hotel compared with where Ella worked, and Kiri had his own room.

Ella knew the hospital had an excellent reputation; once she'd satisfied herself that Kiri was getting the care and attention he needed, she intended to slide into the background and leave everyone to it.

There was no reason for her to be the one palpating Kiri's abdomen to see if his liver was enlarged, while waiting to see if Kiri's blood test results supported the dengue diagnosis. Hmm, it was a little tender. But that wasn't a crisis and she didn't need to do anything *else* herself.

The blood tests came back, with the dengue virus detected. Plus a low white cell count, low platelets and high haematocrit—the measurement of the percentage of red blood cells to the total blood volume—which could indicate potential plasma leakage. Serious, but, as long as you knew what you were dealing with, treatable. He was still drinking, there were no signs of respiratory distress. So far, so good.

*Hands off, Ella, leave it to the staff.*

But… There was no problem in asking for a truckle to be set up for her in Kiri's room, was there? At her hospital, the kids' families always stayed with them for the duration.

So all right, she wasn't family, but his family wasn't here. And kids liked to have people they knew with them. And Ella knew Kiri. Plus, she was making it easier for his nanny to take a break.

She'd got Aaron's cell number from Jenny, and was constantly on the verge of calling him. Only the thought of how many panicked messages he already had waiting for him stopped her. And the tiny suspicion that Aaron would tell her she wasn't needed, which she didn't want to hear—and she hoped that didn't mean she was becoming obsessive about his son.

By the time she'd started haranguing the doctors for updated blood test results, double-checking the nurses' perfect records of Kiri's urine output, heart and respiratory rates, and blood pressure, taking over the task of sponging Kiri down to lower his fever and cajoling him into drinking water and juice to ensure he didn't get dehydrated, she realised she was a step *beyond* obsessive.

It wasn't like she didn't have enough to do at her own place of work, but she couldn't seem to stop herself standing watch over Kiri James like some kind of sentinel—even though dashing between two hospitals was running her ragged.

Kiri's fever subsided on his third day in hospital—but Ella knew better than to assume that meant he was better because often that heralded a critical period. The blood tests with the dropping platelet levels, sharply rising white cells and decreasing haematocrit certainly weren't indicating recovery.

And, suddenly, everything started to go wrong.

Kiri grew increasingly restless and stopped drinking, and Ella went into hyper-vigilant mode.

His breathing became too rapid. His pulse too fast. Even more worryingly, his urine output dropped down to practically nothing.

Ella checked his capillary refill time, pressing on the underside of Kiri's heel and timing how long it took to go from blanched to normal: more than six seconds, when it should only take three.

His abdomen was distended, which indicated

ascites—an accumulation of fluid in the abdominal cavity. 'I'm just going to feel your tummy, Kiri,' she said, and pressed as gently as she could.

He cried out. 'Hurts, Ella.'

'I'm so sorry, darling,' she said, knowing they needed to quickly determine the severity of plasma leakage. 'You need some tests, I'm afraid, so I'm going to call your nurse.'

Ella spoke to the nurse, who raced for the doctor, who ordered an abdominal ultrasound to confirm the degree of ascites and a chest X-ray to determine pleural effusion, which would lead to respiratory distress.

'As you know, Ella,' the doctor explained, drawing her outside, 'a critical amount of plasma leakage will indicate he's going into shock, so we're moving Kiri to the ICU, where we can monitor him. We'll be starting him on intravenous rehydration. We'd expect a fairly rapid improvement, in which case we'll progressively reduce the IV fluids, or they could make the situation worse. No improvement and a significant decrease in haematocrit could suggest internal bleeding, and at that stage we'd look at a blood transfusion. But we're nowhere near that stage so no need to worry. I'll call his father now.'

'Aaron's phone's not working,' Ella said mechanically.

'It is now. He called to tell us he's on his way. I know you're a close friend of the family, so...'

But Ella had stopped listening. She nodded. Murmured a word here and there. Took nothing in.

The doctor patted her arm and left. The orderly would be arriving to take Kiri to ICU. This was it. Over. She wasn't needed any more. And she knew, really, that she had never been needed— the hospital had always had everything under control.

Ella braced herself and went to Kiri's bedside. 'Well, young man,' she said cheerfully, 'you're going somewhere special—ICU.'

'I see you too.'

Ella felt such a rush of love, it almost choked her. 'Hmm. In a way that's exactly what it is. It's where the doctors can see you every minute, until nobody has to poke you in the tummy any more. Okay?'

'Are you coming?'

'No, darling. Someone better is coming. The best surprise. Can you guess who?'

Kiri's eyes lit up. 'Dad?'

'Yep,' she said, and leaned over to kiss him.

The door opened. The orderly. 'And they'll be putting a special tube into you here,' she said, touching his wrist. 'It's superhero juice, so you're going to look like Superman soon. Lucky you!'

A moment later Ella was alone, gathering her few possessions.

Back to reality, she told herself. Devoting her time to where it was really needed, rather than wasting it playing out some mother fantasy.

Ella felt the tears on her cheeks. Wiped them away. Pulled herself together.

Walked super-slowly out of the room.

Ella was the first person he saw.

Aaron was sweaty, frantic. Racing into the hospital. And there she was, exiting. Cool. Remote.

He stopped.

*If Ella is here, Kiri will be all right.* The thought darted into his head without permission. The relief was immediate, almost overwhelming.

A split second later it all fell into place: Ella was the nurse who had spoken to Rebecca. His two worlds colliding. Ex-wife and mother of his child connecting with the woman he wanted to sleep with.

No-go zone.

He reached Ella in three, unthinking strides. 'It was you, wasn't it?'

His sudden appearance before her startled her. But she looked at him steadily enough, with her wedding face on. 'What was me?'

'You spoke to Rebecca.'

'Yes. Jenny handed me the phone. I wasn't going to hang up on a worried parent. I had no *reason* to hang up on her.'

'What did you tell her?'

She raised an eyebrow at him. 'That you and I were having a torrid affair.'

She looked at him, waiting for something.

He looked back—blank.

'Seriously?' she demanded. '*Seriously?*' She shook her head in disgust. 'I told her what I knew about dengue fever, you idiot. That it was a complex illness, and things did go wrong—but that it was relatively simple to treat. I shared my own experience so that she understood. I said that early detection followed by admission to a good hospital almost guaranteed a positive outcome. I explained that, more than anything else, it was a matter of getting the fluid intake right and treating complications as they arose.'

'Oh. I—I don't—'

'I told her Kiri was handling everything bravely enough to break your heart, and that Jenny and I were taking shifts to make sure he had someone familiar with him at all times. I didn't ask her why she wasn't hotfooting it out here, despite the fact that her son was in a lot of pain, with his joints aching and his muscles screaming, and asking for her, for you, constantly.'

'I—'

'Not interested, Aaron.'

'But just—he's all right, isn't he? In ICU, right?'

A look. Dismissive. And then she did that slow walk away.

'Wait a minute!' he exploded.

But Ella only waved an imperious hand—not even bothering to turn around to do it—and kept to her path.

# CHAPTER SIX

WELL…IT BOTHERED Aaron.

Ella's saunter off as though he wasn't even worth talking to.

Followed by Jenny's report of Ella's tireless care: that Ella had begged and badgered the staff and hadn't cared about anyone but his son; the fact that she of all people had been the only one capable of reassuring Rebecca.

He had to keep things simple.

But how simple could it be, when he *knew* Ella would be visiting Kiri—and that when she did, he would have to tell her that, all things considered, she would have to stay away from his son.

Two days. The day Kiri got out of ICU. That's how long it took her.

Aaron had left Kiri for fifteen minutes to grab something to eat, and she was there when he got back to Kiri's room, as though she'd timed it to coincide with his absence.

It wrenched him to see the look on Ella's face as she smoothed Kiri's spiky black hair back from his forehead. To experience again that strange combination of joy and terror that had hit him when he'd seen her coming out of the hospital.

He would *not* want her. He had enough on his plate. And if Ella thought she got to pick and choose when their lives could intersect and when they couldn't—well, no! That was all. No.

She looked up. Defensive. Defiant. *Anxious?*

And he felt like he was being unfair.

And he was *never* unfair.

No wonder she made him so mad. She was changing his entire personality, and not for the better.

After a long, staring moment Ella turned back to Kiri. 'I'll see you a little later, Kiri. Okay?' And then she walked slowly away.

Kiri blinked at his father sleepily, then smiled. 'Where's Ella gone?'

'Back to her hospital. They need her there now. And you've got me.'

Kiri nodded.

He was out of danger, but he looked so tired. 'Are you okay, Kiri? What do you need?'

'Nothing. My head was hurting. And my tummy. And my legs. But Ella fixed me.'

'That's good. But I'm here now.'

'And I was hot. Ella cooled me down.'

'How did she do that?'

'With water and a towel.'

'I can do that for you, sport.'

'I'm not hot any more.' Kiri closed his eyes for a long moment, then blinked them open again and held out his skinny forearm, showing off the small sticking plaster. 'Look,' he said.

'You were on a drip, I know.'

'Superhero juice, Ella said.'

'To get you better.'

A few minutes more passed. 'Dad?'

'What is it, sport?'

'Where's Ella?'

Aaron bit back a sigh. 'She has a lot of people to look after. I'm back now. And Mum will be coming soon.'

'Mum's coming?'

'Yes, she'll be here soon.'

Kiri's eyes drifted shut.

The elation at knowing Kiri was out of danger was still with him. Even the prospect of calling Rebecca again to reinforce his demand that she get her butt on a plane didn't daunt him—although he hoped that, this time, Rebecca wouldn't be off her face.

Of course, breaking the other news to her—that he and Kiri would be heading to LA for his audition after Kiri's convalescence, and then straight on to London—might set off a whole new word of pain. He knew Rebecca was going to hate the confirmation that Aaron had landed both the audition and a plum role in Brand's film, because she resented every bit of career success that came his way.

He suspected she would try to guilt him into leaving Kiri in Sydney with her, just to punish him—for Kiri's illness and for the role in Brand's film—but that wasn't going to happen. Until Rebecca got herself clean, where he went, Kiri went.

So he would call Rebecca, get her travel arrangements under way so she could spend time with Kiri while he got his strength back, and tell her that London was all systems go.

Then he would have only two things to worry about: Kiri's convalescence; and figuring out how to forget Ella Reynolds and the way she had looked at his son.

* * *

Rebecca wasn't coming.

It was a shock that she would forego spending time with Kiri, knowing she wouldn't see him for months.

Aaron was trying to find the right words to say to Kiri and had been tiptoeing around the subject for a while.

The last thing he needed was Ella breezing in—triggering that aggravating, inexplicable and entirely inappropriate sense of relief.

Not that she spared Aaron as much as a look.

'You don't need to tell me how you are today,' she said to Kiri, leaning down to kiss his forehead. 'Because you look like a superhero. I guess you ate your dinner last night! And are you weeing? Oops—am I allowed to say that in front of Dad?'

Kiri giggled, and said, 'Yes,' and Ella gave his son that blinding smile that was so gut-churningly amazing.

She looked beautiful. Wearing a plain, white cotton dress and flat leather tie-up sandals, toting an oversized canvas bag—nothing special about any of it. But she was so…lovely.

She presented Kiri with a delicately carved

wooden dragonfly she'd bought for him at the local market and showed him how to balance it on a fingertip.

Then Kiri asked her about the chicken game she'd told him about on a previous visit.

'Ah—you mean Chab Kon Kleng. Okay. Well they start by picking the strongest one—that would be you, Kiri—to be the hen.'

'But I'm a boy.'

'The rooster, then. And you're like your dad— you're going to defend your kids. And all your little chickens are hiding behind you, and the person who is the crow has to try and catch them, while everyone sings a special song. And, no, I'm not singing it. I'm a terrible singer, and my Khmer is not so good.'

'You asked me something about *ch'heu*. That's Khmer.'

'Yes—I was asking if you were in pain and forgot you were a little Aussie boy.'

'I'm Cambodian too.'

'Yes, you are. Lucky you,' Ella said softly.

Aaron was intrigued at this side of Ella. Sweet, animated, fun.

She glanced at him—finally—and he was surprised to see a faint blush creep into her cheeks.

She grabbed the chart from the end of Kiri's bed, scanning quickly. 'You will be out of here in no time if you keep this up.' Another one of those smiles. 'Anyway, I just wanted to call in and say hello today, but I'll stay longer next time.'

'Next time,' Kiri piped up, 'you'll see Mum. She's coming.'

'Hey—that's great,' she replied.

Aaron sucked in a quick, silent breath. Okay, this was the moment to tell Kiri that Rebecca wasn't coming, and to tell Ella that she wasn't welcome. 'Er…' *Brilliant start.*

Two pairs of eyes focused on him. Curious. Waiting.

Aaron perched on the side of Kiri's bed. 'Mate,' he said, 'I'm afraid Mum still can't leave home, so we're going to have to do without her.'

Kiri stared at him, taking in the news in his calm way.

'But she knows you're almost better, and so you'll forgive her,' Aaron continued. 'And I have to give you a kiss and hug from her—yuckerama.'

Kiri giggled then. 'You always kiss and hug me.'

'Then I guess I can squeeze in an extra when nobody's looking.'

'Okay.'

'Right,' Ella said cheerily. 'You'd better get yourself out of here, young man, so you can get home to Mom. You know what that means— eat, drink, do what the doctor tells you. Now, I'm sure you and Dad have lots to plan so I'll see you later.'

*That* smile at Kiri.

The usual smile—the one minus the eye glow—for him.

And she was gone before Aaron could gather his thoughts.

*See you later*? No, she would *not*.

With a quick 'Back soon' to Kiri, Aaron ran after her.


'Ella, wait.'

Ella stopped, stiffened, turned.

'Can we grab a coffee?'

Ella thought about saying no. She didn't want to feel that uncomfortable mix of guilt and attraction he seemed to bring out in her. But a 'no' would be an admission that he had some kind of power over her, and that would never do. So she nodded and walked beside him to the hospital café, and sat in silence until their coffee was on the table in front of them.

'I wanted to explain. About Rebecca.' He was stirring one sugar into his coffee about ten times longer than he needed to.

'No need,' she said.

'It's just she had an audition, and because Kiri was out of danger...'

She nodded. 'And he'd probably be ready to go home by the time she arrived anyway...'

Aaron looked morosely at the contents in his cup, and Ella felt an unwelcome stab of sympathy.

'Actually, the audition wasn't the main issue,' he said. 'I know the director. He would have held off for her.'

Ella waited while he gave his coffee another unnecessary stir.

'Has Tina told you about Rebecca?' he asked, looking across at her.

'Told me what?'

'About her drug problem?'

'Ah. No. I didn't know. I'm sorry.' That explained the not-really-divorced divorce; Sir Galahad wasn't the type to cut and run in an untenable situation.

'Things are…complicated,' he said. 'Very.'

'I'm sure.'

'It doesn't mean Rebecca isn't anxious about Kiri. I mean, she's his mother, and she loves him.'

'I understand. But he should recover quickly now. At this stage—the recovery phase—all those fluids that leaked out of his capillaries are simply being reabsorbed by his body. Like a wave—flooding, receding, balancing. But he'll be tired for a while. And there may be a rash. Red and itchy, with white centres. Don't freak out about it. Okay?'

Silence. Another stir of the coffee.

'Are you going to drink that, or are you just going to stir it to death?' Ella asked, and then it hit her: this was not really about Rebecca. 'Or… do you want to just tell me what this all has to do with me?'

Aaron looked at her. Kind of determined and apologetic at the same time. 'It's just…he's very attached to you. *Too* attached to you. I don't know how, in such a short time, but he is.'

'It's an occupational hazard for doctors and nurses.'

'No, Ella. It's you. And that makes things more complicated, given he won't be seeing you again once we leave the hospital. I—I don't want him to miss you.'

'Ahhh,' she said, and pushed her cup away. 'I see. Things are complicated, and he already has a mother, so stay away, Ella.'

'It's just the flip side of what you said to me—that you don't like saying goodbye to a child when a relationship goes south.'

'We don't have a relationship. And the fact you're a father didn't seem to bother you when you were kissing me, as long as we weren't *in* a "relationship".'

'Don't be naïve, Ella. It's one thing for us to have sex. It's another when there are two of us sitting together at my son's bedside.'

The hurt took her by surprise. 'So let me get this straight—you're happy to sleep with me, but you don't want me anywhere near your son?'

'We haven't slept together.'

'That's right—we haven't. And calm yourself, we won't. But the principle is still there: it would be *okay* for you to have sex with me, but because you *want* to have sex with me, it's *not* okay for me to be anywhere near your son. And don't throw back at me what I said about not wanting to get mixed up with a man with a kid—which would be my problem to deal with, not yours. Or tell me it's to protect him from the pain of missing me either. Because this is about *you*. This is because *you're* not comfortable around me. I'd go so far as to say you disapprove of me.'

'I don't know what to think of you.' He dragged a hand through his hair. 'One minute you're letting a drunk guy in a bar paw you and the next you're hovering like a guardian angel over sick kids. One minute you're a sarcastic pain in the butt, and the next you're crying like your heart's breaking. Do I approve of you? I don't even know. It's too hard to know you, Ella. Too hard.'

'And you're a saint by comparison, are you? No little flaws or contradictions in your character? So how do you explain your attraction to someone like me?'

'I don't explain it. I can't. That's the problem.' He stopped, closed his eyes for a fraught moment. 'Look, I've got Rebecca to worry about. And Kiri to shield from all that's going on with her. That's why I told you I couldn't develop a relationship with you. To make it cl—'

'I told *you* I didn't want one. Or are you too arrogant to believe that?'

'Wake up, Ella. If Kiri has developed an affec-

tion for you, that means we're *in* a relationship.
Which would be fine if I didn't—'

'Oh, shut up and stir your coffee! This is no
grand passion we're having.' Ella was almost
throbbing with rage, made worse by having to
keep her voice low. A nice yelling match would
have suited her right now but you didn't yell at
people in Cambodia.

She leaned across the table. 'Understand this:
I'm not interested in you. I'm not here, after having worked a very long day, to see you. I'm here
to see Kiri, who was in this hospital parentless.
No father. No mother. Just a nanny. And me.
Holding his hand while they drew his blood for
tests. Coaxing him to drink. Trying to calm him
when he vomited, when his stomach was hurting
and there was no relief for the pain. Knowing his
head was splitting and that paracetamol couldn't
help enough. So scared he'd start bleeding that I
was beside myself because what the hell were we
going to do if he needed a transfusion and you
weren't here? How dare you tell me after that to
stay away from him, like I'm out to seduce you
and spoil your peace and wreck your family?'

She could feel the tears ready to burst, and
dashed a hand across her eyes.

He opened his mouth.

'Just shut *up*,' she said furiously. 'You know, I'm not overly modest about my assets, but I somehow think a fine upstanding man like you could resist making mad passionate love to a bottom feeder like me in front of Kiri, so I suggest you just get over yourself and stop projecting.'

'Projecting?'

'Yes—your guilty feelings on me! I have enough guilt of my own to contend with without you adding a chunky piece of antique furniture to the bonfire. It's not my fault your wife is a drug addict. It's not my fault you got a divorce. It's not my fault your son got dengue fever. It's not my fault you find me attractive, or a distraction, or whatever. I am not the cause or the catalyst or the star of your documentary, and I didn't ask you to lurk around hospital corners, watching me.'

She stood, pushing her chair back violently. 'I'm no saint, but I'm not a monster either.'

She headed for the door at a cracking pace, Aaron scrambling to catch up with her.

He didn't reach her until she was outside, around the corner from the hospital entrance.

'Wait just a minute,' he said, and spun her to face him.

'This conversation is over. Leave me *alone*,' she said, and jerked free, turned to walk off.

His hand shot out, grabbed her arm, spun her back. 'Oh, no, you don't,' he said, and looked as furious as she felt. 'You are not running off and pretending I'm the only one with a problem. Go on, lie to me—tell me you don't want me to touch you.'

He wrenched her up onto her toes and smacked her into his chest. Looked at her for one fierce, burning moment, and then kissed her as though he couldn't help himself.

In a desperate kind of scramble, her back ended up against the wall and he was plastered against her. He took her face between his hands, kissed her, long and hard. 'Ella,' he whispered against her lips. 'Ella. I know it's insane but when you're near me I can't help myself. Can't.'

Ella was tugging his shirt from his jeans, her hands sliding up his chest. 'Just touch me. Touch me!'

His thighs nudged hers apart and he was there, hard against her. She strained against him, ready, so ready, so—

Phone. Ringing. His.

They pulled apart, breathing hard. Looked at each other.

Aaron wrenched the phone from his pocket. Rebecca.

The phone rang. Rang. Rang. Rang. Stopped.

And still Ella and Aaron stared at each other.

Ella swallowed. 'No matter what you think of me—or what I think of myself right now, which isn't much—I don't want to make things difficult. For you, for Kiri. Or for me.' She smoothed her hands down her dress, making sure everything was in order. 'So you win. I'll stay away.'

'Maybe there's another way to—'

Ella cut him off. 'No. We've both got enough drama in our lives without making a fleeting attraction into a Shakespearean tragedy. I just...' Pause. Another swallow. 'I don't want him to think I don't care about him. Because he might think that, when I don't come back.'

Aaron pushed a lock of her hair behind her ear. It was a gentle gesture that had her ducking away. 'That's not helping,' she said.

'Don't think I don't know how lucky I am to have had you watching over Kiri. He knows and

I know that you care about him. And I know how much, after Sann—'

'Don't you dare,' she hissed. 'I should never have told you. I regret it more than I can say. So we'll make a deal, shall we? I'll stay away and you don't ever, *ever* mention Sann again, not to anyone. I don't need or want you to feel sorry for me. I don't need or want *you*. So let's focus on a win-win. You go home. I'll go…wherever. And we'll forget we ever met.'

Ella walked away, but it was harder than it had ever been to slow her steps.

The sooner Aaron James was back in Sydney the better.

She was putting Sydney at number three thousand and one on her list of holiday destinations—right after Afghanistan.

# CHAPTER SEVEN

'ELLA!'

Tina was staring at her. Surprised, delighted. 'Oh, come in. Come in! I'm so glad you're here. I was wondering when you'd use that ticket. Brand,' she called over her shoulder.

Ella cast appreciative eyes over the grand tiled entrance hall of her sister's Georgian townhouse. 'Nice one, Mrs. McIntyre,' she said.

Tina laughed. 'Yes, "nice".'

'So I'm thinking space isn't a problem.'

'We have *oodles* of it. In fact, we have other g—. Oh, here's Brand. Brand, Ella's here.'

'Yes, so I see. Welcome,' Brand said, pulling Tina backwards against his chest and circling her with his arms.

Ella looked at Brand's possessive hands on Tina's swollen belly. In about a month she would be an aunt. She was happy for her sister, happy she'd found such profound love. But looking at this burgeoning family made her heart ache with the memory of what she'd lost, what she might never have.

Not that Ella remembered the love between her and Javier being the deep, absorbing glow that Tina and Brand shared. It had been giddier. A rush of feeling captured in a handful of memories. That first dazzling sight of him outside a makeshift hospital tent in Somalia. Their first tentative kiss. The sticky clumsiness of the first and only time they'd made love—the night before the malaria had hit her; two nights before he was taken.

Would it have grown into the special bond Tina and Brand had? Or burned itself out?

Standing in this hallway, she had never felt so unsure, so…empty. And so envious she was ashamed of herself. Maybe it had been a mistake to come. 'If you'll show me where to dump my stuff, I'll get out of your hair for a couple of hours.'

Tina looked dismayed. 'But I *want* you in my hair.'

'I'm catching up with someone.'

'Who? And where?'

Ella raised her eyebrows.

Tina made an exasperated sound. 'Oh, don't get all frosty.'

Ella rolled her eyes. 'She's a nurse, living in Hammersmith. We're meeting at a pub called the Hare and something. Harp? Carp? Does it matter? Can I go? Please, please, pretty please?'

Tina disentangled herself from her laughing husband's arms. 'All right, you two, give it a rest,' she said. 'Brand—show Ella her room. Then, Ella, go ahead and run away. But I don't expect to have to ambush you every time I want to talk to you.'

Ella kissed Tina's cheek. 'I promise to bore you rigid with tales of saline drips and bandage supplies and oxygen masks. By the time I get to the bedpan stories, you'll be begging me to go out.'

London in summer, what was there not to like? Aaron thought as he bounded up the stairs to Brand's house with Kiri on his back.

He went in search of Brand and Tina and found them in the kitchen, sitting at the table they used for informal family dining.

'Good news! We've found an apartment to rent,' he announced, swinging Kiri down to the floor.

Tina swooped on Kiri to kiss and tickle him, then settled him on the chair beside her with a glass of milk and a cookie. She bent an unhappy look on her husband. 'Why do all our house guests want to run away the minute they step foot in the place?'

'We've been underfoot for two weeks!' Aaron protested. 'And we're only moving down the street.'

'It's her sister,' Brand explained. 'Ella arrived today, stayed just long enough to drop her bag and ran off to some ill-named pub. Princess Tina is *not* amused.'

Aaron's heart stopped—at least that's what it felt like—and then jump-started violently. He imagined himself pale with shock, his eyes bugging out. He felt his hair follicles tingle. What had they said while he'd been sitting there stunned? What had he missed? He forced himself to take a breath, clear his mind, concentrate. Because the only coalescing thought in his head was that she was here. In London. In this house.

He'd thought he would never see her again. Hadn't wanted to see her again.

But she was here.

'…when we weren't really expecting her,' Tina said.

*Huh? What? What had he missed while his brain had turned to mush?*

'You know what she's like,' Brand said.

*What?* What's *she like?* Aaron demanded silently.

'What do you mean, what she's like?' Tina asked, sounding affronted.

*Bless you, Tina.*

'Independent. Very,' Brand supplied. 'She's used to looking after herself. And she's been in scarier places. Somehow I think she'll make it home tonight just fine.'

'Yes, but what time? And she hasn't even told me how long she's staying. Mum and Dad are going to want a report. How can I get the goss if she runs away when she should be talking to me?'

Brand gave her a warning look. 'If you fuss, she *will* go.' He turned to Aaron, changing the subject. 'So, Aaron, when do you move in?'

'A week,' Aaron said, racking his brain for a way to get the conversation casually back to Ella. 'Is that all right? I mean, if your sister is here...' he looked back at Tina '...maybe Kiri and I should leave earlier.' He'd lost it, obviously, because as the words left his mouth he wanted to recall them. 'We can easily move to a hotel.' Nope. That wasn't working for him either.

He caught himself rubbing his chest, over

his heart. Realised it wasn't the first time he'd thought of Ella and done that.

'No way—you're not going any earlier than you have to,' Tina said immediately, and Aaron did the mental equivalent of swooning with relief.

And that really hit home.

The problem wasn't that he didn't want to see Ella—it was that he did.

On his third trip downstairs that night, Aaron faced the fact that he was hovering. He hadn't really come down for a glass of water. Or a book. Or a midnight snack.

Barefoot, rumpled, and edgy, he had come down looking for Ella.

On his fourth trip he gave up any pretence and took a seat in the room that opened off the dimly lit hall—a library-cum-family room. From there he could hear the front door open and yet be hidden. He turned on only one lamp; she wouldn't even know he was there, if he chose the sensible option and stayed hidden when the moment came.

He was, quite simply, beside himself.

Aaron helped himself to a Scotch, neat, while he waited. His blood pressure must have been skyrocketing, because his heart had been thumping away at double speed all day.

And he had *excellent* blood pressure that *never* skyrocketed.

He knew precisely how long he'd been waiting—an hour and thirteen minutes—when he heard it.

Key hitting the lock. Lock clicking. Door opening.

A step on the tiled floor. He took a deep breath. Tried—failed—to steady his nerves. Heard the door close. Then nothing. No footsteps. A long moment passed. And then another sound. Something slumping against the wall or the door or the floor.

Was she hurt? Had she fallen?

Another sound. A sort of hiccup that wasn't a hiccup. A hitched breath.

He got to his feet and walked slowly to the door. Pushed it open silently. How had he ever thought he might sit in here and *not* go to her? And then he saw her and almost gasped! He was so monumentally unprepared for the punch of lust that hit him as he peered out like a thief.

She was sitting on the floor. Back against the door, knees up with elbows on them, hands jammed against her mouth. He could have sworn she was crying but there were no tears.

He saw the complete stillness that came into her as she realised someone was there.

And then she looked up.

# CHAPTER EIGHT

AARON WALKED SLOWLY towards Ella. She was wearing a dark green skirt that had fallen up her thighs. A crumpled white top with a drawstring neckline. Leather slide-on sandals. Her hair was in loose waves, long, hanging over her shoulders—he'd never seen it loose before.

He felt a tense throb of some emotion he couldn't name, didn't want to name, as he reached her. He stood looking down at her, dry-mouthed. 'Where have you been?' he asked.

'Why are you here?' she countered, the remembered huskiness of her voice scattering his thoughts for a moment.

The way her skirt was draping at the top of her thighs was driving him insane. *Concentrate.* 'Here? I've been staying here. I'm working here. In London, I mean. Brand's film.' He couldn't even swallow. 'Didn't they tell you?'

'No,' Ella said, sighing, and easily, gracefully, got to her feet. 'Well, that's just great. I guess you're going to expect me to move out now, so I don't corrupt Kiri—or you.'

'No. I don't want you to move out. We'll be leaving in a week, anyway.'

'Oh, that makes me feel *so* much better. I'm sure I can avoid doing anything too immoral for one lousy week.'

Her silky skirt had settled back where it was supposed to be. It was short, so he could still see too much of her thighs. He jerked his gaze upwards and it collided with her breasts. He could make out the lace of her bra, some indistinguishable pale colour, under the white cotton of her top.

His skin had started to tighten and tingle, so he forced his eyes upwards again. Jammed his hands in his pockets as he caught the amused patience in her purple eyes.

'Why are you waiting up for me?' she asked.

He had no answer.

She sighed again—an exaggerated, world-weary sigh. 'What do you want, Aaron?'

'I want you,' he said. He couldn't quite believe he'd said it after everything that had gone on between them, but once it was out it seemed so easy. So clear. As though he hadn't spent agonising weeks telling himself she was the *last* thing he needed in his life and he'd been right to put the brakes on in Cambodia. 'I haven't stopped wanting you. Not for a second.'

Her eyebrows arched upwards. Even her eyebrows were sexy.

'I think we've been through this already, haven't we?' she asked softly, and started to move past him. 'One week—I'm sure you can resist me for that long, Sir Galahad.'

His hand shot out. He saw it move, faster than his brain was working. Watched his fingers grip her upper arm.

She turned to face him.

He didn't know what he intended to do next— but at least she wasn't looking amused any more.

She looked hard at him for a moment. And then she took his face between her hands and kissed him, fusing her mouth to his with forceful passion. She finished the kiss with one long lick against his mouth. Pulled back a tiny fraction, then seemed to change her mind and kissed him again. Pulled back. Stepped back. Looked him in the eye.

'Now what?' she asked, her breathing unsteady but her voice controlled. 'This is where you run away, isn't it? Because of Rebecca. Or Kiri. Or just because it's me.'

That strange other being still had control of him. It was the only explanation for the way he jerked her close, crushed his arms around her and kissed her. He broke the contact only for a second at a time. To breathe. He wished he didn't even have to stop for that. His hands were everywhere, couldn't settle. In her hair, on her back, gripping her bottom, running up her sides. And through it all he couldn't seem to stop kissing her.

He could hear her breathing labouring, like his. When his hands reached her breasts, felt the nipples jutting into his palms through two layers of clothing, he shuddered. He finally stopped kissing her, but kept his mouth on hers, still, reaching for control. 'Now what?' He repeated her question without moving his mouth from hers, after a brief struggle to remember what she'd asked. Kissed her again.

Ella wrapped her arms around his waist and he groaned. He looked down into her face. 'There doesn't seem to be much point in running away, because you're always there. So now, Ella, I get to have you.'

One long, fraught moment of limbo.

He didn't know what he'd do if she said no, he was so on fire for her.

But she didn't say no. She said, 'Okay. Let's be stupid, then, and get it done.'

Not exactly a passionate acquiescence, but he'd take it. Take her, any way he could get her.

He kissed her again, pulling her close, letting her feel how hard he was for her, wanting her to know. Both of his hands slipped into her hair. It was heavy, silky. Another time he would like to stroke his fingers through it, but not now. Now he was too desperate. He dragged fistfuls of it, using it to tilt her head back, anchoring her so he could kiss her harder still. 'Come upstairs,' he breathed against her mouth. 'Come with me.'

'All yours,' Ella said in that mocking way she had—but Aaron didn't care. He grabbed her hand and walked quickly to the staircase, pulling her up it at a furious pace.

'Which way to your room?' he asked.

Silently, she guided him to it.

The room next to his.

Fate.

The moment they were inside he was yanking her top up and over her head, fumbling with her skirt until it lay pool-like at her feet. The bedside lamp was on and he said a silent prayer of thanks because it meant he could see her. She stood before him in pale pink underwear so worn it was almost transparent, tossing her hair back over her shoulders. He swallowed. He wanted to rip her underwear to shreds to get to her. It was like a madness. Blood pounding through his veins, he stripped off his T-shirt and shoved his jeans and underwear off roughly.

She was watching him, following what he was doing as she kicked off her sandals. Aaron forced himself to stand still and let her see him. He hoped she liked what she saw.

Ella came towards him and circled his biceps with her hands—at least, partly; his biceps were too big for her to reach even halfway around. Aaron remembered that she liked tattoos. His tattooed armbands were broad and dark and intricately patterned—and, yes, she clearly did like what she saw. The tattoos had taken painful hours to complete and, watching her eyes light up as she touched them, he'd never been happier to have them. He hoped during the night she would see the more impressive tattoo on his back, but he couldn't imagine taking his eyes off her long enough to turn around.

He couldn't wait any longer to see her naked. He reached for her hips, and she obligingly released his arms and stepped closer. She let him push her panties down, stepped free of them when they hit the floor. Then she let him work the back fastening of her bra as she rested against him, compliant. As he wrestled with the bra, he could feel her against him, thigh to thigh, hip to hip. The tangle of soft hair against his erection had his heart bashing so hard and fast in his chest he thought he might have a coronary. Oh, he liked the feel of it. She was perfect. Natural and perfect. His hands were shaking so badly as he tried to undo her bra he thought he was going to have to tear it off, but it gave at last. Her breasts, the areoles swollen, nipples sharply erect, pressed into his chest as he wrenched the bra off. He was scared to look at her in case he couldn't stop himself falling on her like a ravening beast...but at the same time he was desperate to see her.

'Ella,' he said, his voice rough as he stepped back just enough to look. With one hand he touched her face. The other moved lower to the dark blonde hair at the apex of her thighs. He combed through it with trembling fingers. Lush and beautiful. He could feel the moisture seeping into it. Longed to taste it. Taste her. He dropped to his knees, kissed her there.

Aaron loved the hitch in her voice as his fingers and tongue continued to explore. 'I do want you, Aaron. Just so you know. Tonight, I do want you,' Ella said, and it was like a flare went off in his head. He got to his feet, dragged her into his arms, holding her close while his mouth dived on hers. He moved the few steps that would enable him to tumble her backwards onto the bed and come down on her.

The moment they hit the bed he had his hands on her thighs and was pushing her legs apart.

'Wait,' she said in his ear. 'Condoms. Bedside table. In the drawer.'

Somehow, Aaron managed to keep kissing her as he fumbled with the drawer, pulled it open and reached inside. His fingers mercifully closed on one quickly—thankfully they were loose in there.

He kissed her once more, long and luscious, before breaking to free the condom from its packaging. Kneeling between her thighs, he smoothed it on, and Ella raised herself on her elbows to watch. She looked irresistibly wicked, and as he finished the job he leaned forward to take one of her nipples in his mouth. She arched forward and gasped and he decided penetration could wait. She tasted divine. Exquisite. The texture of her was maddeningly good, the feel of her breasts as he held them in his hands heavy and firm. He could keep his mouth on her for hours, he thought, just to hear the sounds coming from her as his tongue circled, licked.

But Ella was shifting urgently beneath him, trying to position him with hands and thighs and the rest of her shuddering body. 'Inside,' she said, gasping. 'Come inside me. Now.'

With one thrust he buried himself in her, and then he couldn't seem to help himself. He pulled back and thrust deeply into her again. And again and again. He was kissing her mouth, her eyes, her neck as he drove into her over and over. The sound of her gasping cries urged him on until he felt her clench around him. She sucked in a breath, whooshed it out. Again. Once more. She was coming, tense and beautiful around him, and he'd never been so turned on in his life. He slid his arms under her on the bed, dragged her up against him and thrust his tongue inside her mouth. And with one last, hard push of his hips he came, hard and strong.

As the last waves of his climax receded, the

fog of pure lust cleared from Aaron's head and he was suddenly and completely appalled.

Had he hurt her? Something primal had overtaken him, and he hadn't felt in control of himself. And he was *never, ever* out of control.

He kissed her, trying for gentleness but seemingly unable to achieve it even now, because the moment his mouth touched hers he was out of control again.

Aaron couldn't seem to steady his breathing. It was somehow beautiful to Ella to know that.

He sure liked kissing. Even now, after he'd exhausted both of them and could reasonably be expected to roll over and go to sleep, he was kissing her. In between those unsteady breaths of his. He seemed to have an obsession with her mouth. Nobody had ever kissed her quite like this before. It was sweet, and sexy as hell, to be kissed like he couldn't stop. It was getting her aroused again. She'd sneered at herself as she'd put those condoms in the drawer, but now all she could think was: did she have enough?

He shifted at last, rolling onto his back beside her. 'Sorry, I know I'm heavy. And you're so slender,' he said.

'It's just the—' She stopped. How did you describe quickly the way long hours, fatigue and illness sapped the calories out of you at breakneck speed? 'Nothing, really. I'm already gaining weight. It happens fast when I'm not working.'

'So you can lose it all over again the next time,' Aaron said, and Ella realised she didn't have to explain after all.

His eyes closed as he reached for her hand.

Okay, so now he'll go to sleep, Ella thought, and was annoyed with herself for bringing him to her room. If they'd gone to his room she could have left whenever she wanted; but what did a woman say, do, to get a man to leave?

But Aaron, far from showing any signs of sleep, brought her hand to his mouth and rolled onto his side, facing her. He released her hand but then pulled her close so that her side was fitted against his front, and nuzzled his nose into the side of her neck. He slid one of his hands down over her belly and between her legs. 'Did I hurt you, Ella?'

*Huh?* 'Hurt me?'

'Yes. I was rough. I'm sorry.'

As he spoke his fingers were slipping gently against the delicate folds of her sex. It was like he was trying to soothe her. Her heart stumbled, just a little, as she realised what he was doing. And he was looking at her so seriously while he did it. He had the most remarkably beautiful eyes. And, of course, he was ridiculously well endowed, but she'd been so hot and ready for him it hadn't hurt. It had been more erotic than anything she could have dreamed.

How did she tell him that his fingers, now, weren't soothing? That what he was doing to her was gloriously *good*, but not soothing?

'No, Aaron, you— Ah…' She had to pause for a moment as the touch of his fingers became almost unbearable. 'I mean, no. I mean, you didn't hurt me.' She paused again. 'Aaron,' she said, almost breathless with desire, 'I suggest you go and get rid of that condom. And then hurry back and get another one.'

He frowned, understanding but wary. 'You're sure? I mean— Oh,' as her hands found him. 'I guess you're sure.' He swung his legs off the side of the bed and was about to stand but Ella, on her knees in an instant, embraced him from behind. Her mouth touched between his shoulder blades then he felt her tongue trace the pattern of the dragon inked across his back.

'I don't want to leave you,' he said huskily. 'Come with me.'

Ella, needing no second invitation, was out of the bed and heading for the en suite bathroom half a step behind him.

Ella trailed the fingers of one hand along his spine and snapped on the light with the fingers of her other. 'Oh, my, it's even better in the full light.'

Aaron discarded the condom and started to turn around. She imagined he thought he was going to take her in his arms.

'No, you don't. It's my turn,' Ella said.

She turned on the shower, drew Aaron in beside her, and as he reached for her again she shook her head, laughing, and dodged out of the way. 'I'm glad this is such a small shower cubicle,' she said throatily. 'Close. Tight.' She spun Aaron roughly to face the tiled wall, slammed him up against it and grabbed the cake of soap from its holder. Lathering her hands, his skin, she plastered herself against his back, moving her breasts sensually against his beautiful tattoo as she reached around to fondle him. 'I love the size of you,' she said, as his already impressive erection grew in her hands. 'I want to take you like this, from behind.'

'I think I'd take you any way I could get you,' Aaron said, groaning as she moved her hands between his legs. He was almost panting and Ella had never felt so beautiful, so powerful.

At last.

She could have this, at last.

As her hands slid, slipped, squeezed, Aaron rested his forehead against the shower wall and submitted.

Aaron watched as Ella slept. She'd fallen into sleep like a stone into the ocean.

No wonder. Aaron had been all over her from the moment they'd left the shower. Inexhaustible. He didn't think he'd understood the word lust until tonight. If he could have breathed her into his lungs, he would have.

He didn't know why he wanted her so badly. But even having had her three times, he couldn't get her close enough. She was in his blood. What a pathetic cliché. But true.

The bedside light was still on, so he could see her face. She looked serious in her sleep. Fretful. Aaron pulled her closer, kissed one of her wickedly arched eyebrows. He breathed in the scent of her hair. Looking at her was almost painful. The outrageous loveliness of her.

Sighing, he turned off the bedside light. It was past five in the morning and he should go back to his room, but he wanted to hold her.

He thought about their last meeting, in Cambodia. The horrible things they'd said to each other. They'd made a pact to forget they'd ever met. How had they gone from that to being here in bed now?

What had he been thinking when he'd left the library, when he'd seen her slumped against the front door with her fists jammed against her mouth?

On a mundane level, he'd thought she must have been drinking. Or maybe he'd hoped that, so he could pigeonhole her back where he'd wanted to.

Oh, he had no doubt she regularly drank to excess—it fitted with the general wildness he sensed in her. But tonight she'd smelled only like that tantalising perfume. And her mouth had tasted like lime, not booze. It was obvious, really, when he pieced together what he knew about her, what he'd seen of her: she wouldn't let Tina see her out of control. She would be sober and serene and together in this house. The way her family expected her to be. The way she'd been described to him before he'd ever met her.

He thought about the day he'd held her as she'd cried over Bourey's death. And the other boy, Sann, whose death had been infinitely painful for her. Things she didn't want anyone to know.

She was so alone. She chose to be, so her fears and sorrows wouldn't hurt anyone else.

Aaron pulled her closer. She roused, smiled sleepily at him. 'You should go,' she said, but then she settled herself against him and closed her eyes, so he stayed exactly where he was.

Wondering how he could both have her and keep things simple.

# CHAPTER NINE

ELLA ROLLED RESTLESSLY, absent-mindedly pulling Aaron's pillow close and breathing in the scent of him, wondering what time he'd left.

She didn't know what had come over her. She'd finally managed to get past second base—way past it, with a blistering home run. And it had been with her brother-in-law's friend under her sister's roof. Not that there had seemed to be much choice about it. It had felt like…well, like fate.

And Aaron wouldn't tell, she reassured herself.

She got out of bed, reached for her robe, and then just sat on the edge of the bed with the robe in her lap. She didn't want to go downstairs. Because downstairs meant reality. It meant Tina and Brand. And Aaron—not Lover Aaron but Friend-of-her-sister Aaron. Daddy Aaron.

She stood slowly and winced a little. It had been a very active night. A fabulous night. But she would have been relieved even if it had been the worst sex of her life instead of the best. Because she had needed it.

Yesterday she'd forced herself to think about Sann. Tina's pregnancy was an immutable fact, and Ella knew she had to come to terms with it; she couldn't run away every time a pang of envy hit her. So she had deliberately taken the memories out of mothballs and examined them one by one. A kind of desensitisation therapy.

But forcing the memories had been difficult. So when she'd come home to find Aaron there, sex with him had offered an escape. A talisman to keep her sad thoughts at bay, hopefully ward off the bad dreams.

She had been prepared to make a bargain with herself—sex and a nightmare-free night, in exchange for guilt and shame today.

And she did feel the guilt.

Just not the shame.

What did that mean?

*Get it together, Ella. It was just a one-night stand. People do it all the time. Simple.*

Except it was *not* simple. Because she hadn't managed it before. And she recalled—too vividly—Aaron walking towards her in the hallway, and how much she'd wanted him as their eyes had met. She was deluding herself if she thought she'd only been interested in a nightmare-free night. Oh, he had certainly materialised at a point when she'd been at her lowest ebb and open to temptation, but she had wanted him, wanted the spark, the flash of almost unbearable attraction that had been there in Cambodia.

But now what?

Nothing had really changed. All the reasons not to be together in Cambodia were still there. Kiri. Rebecca. Javier.

*Definitely* time to return to reality.

Ella tossed the robe aside and strode into the bathroom.

She looked at herself in the mirror. Her mouth looked swollen. Nothing she could do to hide that, except maybe dab a bit of foundation on it to minimise the rawness. She could see small bruises on her upper arms—easily covered. There were more bruises on her hips, but nobody would be seeing those. She sucked in a breath as more memories of the night filled her head. Aaron had been insatiable—and she had loved it. She had more than a few sore spots. And, no doubt, so did he. Like the teeth marks she'd left on his inner thigh.

Ella caught herself smiling. Aaron had called her a vampire, but he hadn't minded. He hadn't minded at all, if the passionate lovemaking that had followed had been any indication.

The smile slipped.

He would have come to his senses by now. Remembered that he didn't like her. Didn't want her near his son.

Time to store the memory and move on.

Tina checked the clock on the kitchen wall as Ella walked in. 'So lunch, not breakfast.'

'Oh, dear, am I going to have to punch a time clock whenever I come and go?'

'Oh, for heaven's sake!'

'Well, sorry, Tina, but really you're as bad as Mom. Just sit down and tell me stories about Brand as a doting father while I make us both something to eat.'

Ella forced herself to look at Tina's stomach as she edged past her sister. Bearable. She could do this.

Tina groaned as she levered herself onto a stool at the kitchen counter. 'I am so over the doting father thing. We've done the practice drive to the hospital seven times. And he's having food cravings. It's not funny, Ella!'

But Ella laughed anyway as she laid a variety of salad vegetables on a chopping board. 'Where is he now?'

'On the set, thank goodness. Which reminds me—I didn't tell you we have other guests.'

*Ah. Control time.* Ella busied herself pulling out drawers.

'What are you looking for?' Tina asked.

Ella kept her head down and pulled open another drawer. 'Knife.'

'Behind you, knife block on the counter,' Tina said, and Ella turned her back on her sister and took her time selecting a knife.

'Where was I?' Tina asked. 'Oh yes, Aaron. Aaron James and his son. You know them, of course.'

Indistinct mumble.

'Aaron is in Brand's movie,' Tina continued. 'That's why he's in London. They've been staying with us, but they're only here for another week.'

'Why's that?' Ella asked, desperately nonchalant, and started chopping as though her life depended on the precision of her knife action.

'Aaron was always intending to find a place of his own, and yesterday he did.'

'So...would it be easier if I moved out for the week? Because I have friends I was going to see and I—'

'What is wrong with you people? Everyone wants to move out. We've got enough room to house a baseball team! And, anyway, I need you to help me look after Kiri.'

*Uh-oh.* 'What? Why?'

'Kiri's nanny had some crisis and can't get here until next week. Aaron's due on set tomorrow so I volunteered. I told him it would be good practice. And Kiri is adorable.'

Ella's hand was a little unsteady so she put down the knife. Kiri. She would be looking after Kiri. Aaron wouldn't want that. 'But what about—? I mean, shouldn't he have stayed in Sydney? With his mother?' *Drugs, Ella, drugs.* 'Or—or...someone?'

Tina looked like she was weighing something up. 'The thing is—oh, I don't know if... Okay, look, this is completely confidential, Ella.'

Tina put up her hands at the look on Ella's face. 'Yes, I know you're a glued-shut clam. Aaron is just sensitive about it. Or Rebecca is, and he's respecting that. Rebecca is in rehab. Drugs. Apparently, she auditioned for a role in a new TV show while Aaron was in Cambodia, but didn't get it. The director told her if she didn't get things under control, she'd never work again.'

'That's…tough. How—how's Kiri coping with the separation?'

'Aaron does all the parenting, so it's not as big a deal as you'd think. He has sole custody. But that's not to say Rebecca doesn't see Kiri whenever she wants. It's just that the drugs have been a problem for some time.'

'Oh. *Sole* custody. Huh.' Ella scooped the chopped salad vegetables into a large bowl. 'But should he…Aaron…should he be here while she's there?'

'Well, they *are* divorced, although sometimes I wonder if Rebecca really believes that. But in any case, it's not a case of him shirking responsibility. Aaron found the clinic—in California, while he was over there auditioning for a new crime show—because Rebecca wanted to do it away from her home city where it might have leaked to the press. And he got her settled in over there, which pushed back filming here so it's all over the place, but what can you do? And of course he's paying, despite having settled a fortune on her during the divorce. He'll be back and forth with Kiri, who thinks it's a spa! But there are strict rules about visiting. Anyway, I hope it works, because Aaron needs to move on, and he won't until Rebecca gets her act together.' She slanted an uncomfortably speculative look at Ella.

'Don't even!' Ella said, interpreting without difficulty.

'Come on, Ella. He's totally, completely hot.'

Ella concentrated on drizzling dressing over the salad.

'Hot as Hades,' Tina said, tightening the thumb-screws. 'But also sweet as heaven. He is amazingly gentle with Kiri. And with me, too. He took me for an ultrasound last week. I had a fall down the stairs and I was petrified.'

Ella hurried to her sister's side, hugged her. 'But everything's all right. You're fine, the baby's fine, right?'

'Yes, but Brand was filming, and I couldn't bring myself to call him. Because I'd already had one fall on the stairs, and he was furious because I was hurrying.'

'Well *stop* hurrying, Tina.' Tentatively, Ella

reached and placed a hand on Tina's stomach. The baby kicked suddenly and Ella's hand jerked away—or would have, if Tina hadn't stopped it, flattened it where it was, kept it there. Tina looked at her sister, wonder and joy in her eyes, and Ella felt her painful envy do a quantum shift.

'So anyway, Aaron,' Tina said. 'He was home. Actually, he saw it happen. I don't know which of us was more upset. He must have cajoled and threatened and who knows what else to get the ultrasound arranged so quickly. He knew it was the only way I'd believe everything was all right. And he let me talk him into not calling Brand until we got the all clear and I was back home.' Tina smiled broadly. 'Unbelievably brave! Brand exploded about being kept in the dark, as Aaron knew he would, but Aaron took it all in his stride. He just let Brand wear himself out, and then took him out for a beer.'

Ella tried not to be charmed, but there was something lovely about the story. 'Well I'm here now to take care of you,' she said, navigating the lump in her throat.

'And I'm very glad.' Tina took Ella's left hand and placed it alongside the right one that was already pressed to her stomach. 'It really scared me, Ella. But I'm not telling you all this to worry you—and don't, whatever you do, tell Mum and Dad.'

'I wouldn't dream of it.'

'I just wanted you to know. I mean, you're my sister! And a nurse. And…well, you're my sister. And I wanted to explain about Aaron. Don't disapprove of him because of Rebecca. He takes his responsibilities very seriously. He practically raised his three young sisters, you know, after his parents died, and he was only eighteen. They idolise him. So does Kiri. And so do I, now. He'll do the right thing by Rebecca, divorced or not, and—more importantly—the right thing by Kiri.'

Ella moved her hands as Tina reached past her to dig into the salad bowl and extract a sliver of carrot.

'You're going to need more than salad, Ella,' Tina said. 'You're like a twig.'

'Yes, yes, yes, I know.' Ella moved back into the food preparation area. 'I'll make some sandwiches.'

'Better make enough for Aaron and Kiri—they should be back any minute.'

For the barest moment Ella paused. Then

she opened the fridge and rummaged inside it. 'Where are they?'

'The park. Aaron's teaching Kiri how to play cricket.'

'Ah,' Ella said meaninglessly, and started slapping various things between slices of bread like she was in a trance.

'Yeah, I think that's enough for the entire Australian and English cricket teams,' Tina said eventually.

'Oh. Sorry. Got carried away.'

*Breathe*, Ella ordered herself when she heard Aaron calling out to Tina from somewhere in the house as she was positioning the platter of sandwiches on the table.

'In the kitchen,' Tina called back.

Tina turned to Ella. 'And I guess you'll tell me later about last night. Probably not fit for children's ears, anyway.'

Ella froze, appalled. Tina *knew*?

'I mean, come on, your mouth,' Tina teased. 'Or are you going to tell me you got stung by a bee?'

'Who got stung by a bee?' Aaron asked, walking in.

# CHAPTER TEN

'OH, NOBODY,' TINA said airily.

But Aaron wasn't looking at Tina. He was looking at Ella.

And from the heat in his eyes Ella figured he was remembering last night in Technicolor detail. Ella felt her pulse kick in response. *Insane.*

'Nice to see you again, Ella,' he said.

Could Tina hear that caress in his voice? Ella frowned fiercely at him.

He winked at her. Winked!

'Kiri can't wait to see you,' he continued. 'He's got a present for you—he's just getting it.'

'Oh, that's— Oh.' She gave up the effort of conversation. She was out of her depth. Shouldn't Aaron be keeping Kiri *away* from her? Ella wondered if Aaron had taken a cricket ball to the head. They were deadly, cricket balls.

Ella was aware a phone was ringing. She noted, dimly, Tina speaking. Sensed Tina leaving the room.

And then Aaron was beside her, taking her hand, lifting it to his mouth, kissing it. The back, the palm. His tongue on her fingers.

'Stop,' she whispered, but the air seemed to have been sucked out of the room and she wasn't really sure the word had left her mouth.

Aaron touched one finger to her swollen bottom lip. 'I'm sorry. Is it sore?'

Ella knocked his hand away. 'What's gotten into you?'

The next moment she found herself pulled into Aaron's arms. 'I've got a solution,' he said, as though she would have *any* idea what he was talking about! Yep, cricket ball to the head.

'A solution for what?'

'You and me. It's based on the KISS principle.'

'The what?'

'KISS: keep it simple, stupid.'

'*Simple* would be to forget last night happened.'

Ella started to pull away, but he tightened his arms.

He rested his forehead on hers. 'Let me. Just for a moment.'

Somehow she found her arms around his waist, and she was just standing there, letting him hold her as though it were any everyday occurrence. *Uh-oh. Dangerous.*

'There's no solution needed for a one-night stand,' she said.

He released her, stepped back. 'I don't want a one-night stand.'

'Um—I think you're a little late to that party.'

'Why?'

'Because we've already had one.'

'So tonight will make it a two-night stand. And tomorrow night a three-night stand, and so on.'

'We agreed, in Cambodia—'

'Cambodia-shmodia.'

'Huh?'

'That was then. This is now.'

'Did you get hit in the head with a cricket ball?'

'What?'

'You're talking like you've got a head injury.'

'It's relief. It's making me light-headed. Because for the first time since Tina and Brand's wedding I know what I'm doing.'

'Well, I don't know what you're doing. I don't think I want to know. I mean, the *KISS* principle?'

'I want you. You want me. We get to have each other. Simple.'

'Um, *not* simple. Kiri? Rebecca? The fact you don't like me? That you don't even know me?'

'Kiri and Rebecca—they're for me to worry about, not you.'

'You're wrong. Tina wants me to help her look after Kiri. Surely you don't want that? Aren't you scared I'll corrupt him or something?'

'Ella, if I know one thing, it's that you would never do anything to hurt Kiri. I've always known it. What I said, in Cambodia...' He shrugged. 'I was being a moron. Projecting, you called it, and you were right. There. I'm denouncing myself.'

'I don't want to play happy families.'

'Neither do I. That's why your relationship with Kiri is separate from my relationship with Kiri, which is separate from my relationship with you. And before you throw Rebecca at me—it's the same deal. You don't even have a relationship with her, so that's purely my issue, not yours.'

'You said the R word. I don't want a relationship—and neither do you.'

Aaron took her hand and lifted it so that it rested on his chest, over his heart. 'Our relationship is going to be purely sexual. Casual sex, that's what you said you wanted. All you were interested in. Well, I can do casual sex.'

'You're not a casual kind of guy, Aaron,' she said.

He smiled, shrugged. 'I'll *make* myself that kind of guy. I said last night I would take you any way I could get you. We're two adults seeking mutual satisfaction and nothing more. An emotion-free zone, which means we can keep it strictly between us—Tina and Brand don't need to know, it's none of Rebecca's business, and Kiri is…well, protected, because your relationship with him is nothing to do with your relationship with me. Simple. Agreed?'

Ella hesitated—not saying yes, but not the automatic 'no' she should be rapping out either. Before she could get her brain into gear, the kitchen door opened.

As Ella pulled her hand free from where, she'd just realised, it was still being held against Aaron's heart, Kiri ran in, saw her, stopped, ran again. Straight at her.

'Kiri, my darling,' she said, and picked him up.

She kissed his forehead. He hugged her, his arms tight around her neck, and didn't seem to want to let go. So she simply moved backwards, with him in her arms, until she felt a chair behind her legs and sat with him on her lap.

Kiri kissed her cheek and Ella's chest tightened dangerously. Kiri removed one arm from around Ella's neck and held out his hand to her. His fist was closed around something.

'What's this?' Ella asked.

Kiri opened his fingers to reveal an unremarkable rock. 'From the beach where you live,' he said. 'Monica.'

Ella smiled at him. 'You remembered?'

Kiri nodded and Ella hugged him close. Santa Monica. He'd been to Santa Monica, and remembered it was where she lived.

She felt a hand on her shoulder and looked up. Aaron was beside her, looking down at her, and she couldn't breathe.

The door opened and Tina breezed in. She paused—an infinitesimal pause—as she took in Aaron's hand on Ella's shoulder, Kiri on her lap.

Aaron slowly removed his hand, but stayed where he was.

'So,' Tina said brightly, 'let's eat.'

Lunch was dreadful.

Kiri was at least normal, chattering away about

Cambodia, about Disneyland, about Sydney, completely at ease.

But Tina was giving off enough gobsmacked vibes to freak Ella out completely.

And Aaron was high-beaming Ella across the table as though he could get her on board with the force of his eyes alone—and if they were really going to carry on a secret affair, he'd have to find his poker face pretty damned fast.

*If?* Was she really going the 'if' route? Not the 'no way' route?

Casual sex.

Could she do it? She'd liked having someone close to her last night. She'd felt alive in a way she hadn't for such a long time. And she hadn't had the dreaded nightmares with Aaron beside her. So. A chance to feel alive again. With no strings attached. No emotions, which she couldn't offer him anyway.

But, ironic though it was, Aaron James seemed to have the ability to make her want to clean up her act. Maybe it was the way he was with Kiri, or that he cared so much about an ex-wife who clearly made his life a misery, or his general tendency to turn into Sir Galahad at regular intervals and save damsels in distress—his sisters, ex-wife, Tina, her.

Whatever the reason, if she wanted to rehabilitate her self-image, was an affair the way to start? Every time she'd let a guy pick her up, determined to do it, just do it and move on, she'd hated herself. Now that she'd gone the whole nine yards, wouldn't she end up hating herself even more? Especially if it became a regular arrangement?

'I'll clear up,' Tina said, when lunch couldn't be stretched out any more.

'Ella and I can manage,' Aaron said quickly.

'No, *Ella and I* can manage,' Tina insisted. She stood and arched her back, grimaced.

Ella got to her feet. 'You should rest,' she told her sister. 'And you…' with an almost fierce look at Aaron '…should get Kiri into bed for a nap. He's sleepy.' She started gathering empty plates.

Aaron looked like he was about to argue so Ella simply turned her back on him and took an armload of plates to the sink. She stayed there, clattering away, refusing to look up, willing him to leave.

And then, at last, Tina spoke. 'The coast is clear. You can come up for air.'

Ella raised her head cautiously and waited for the inevitable.

'What's going on?' Tina asked simply.

'If you mean between me and Aaron, nothing.'

'Of course I mean you and Aaron. He's gaga. It's so obvious.'

'He's not *gaga*.'

'Oh, I beg to differ.'

'We just… We just got to know each other in Cambodia. I called in to check on Kiri a few times when he was ill with dengue fever and Aaron was out in the field, so he's…grateful. I guess.'

Tina snorted out a laugh. 'If that's gratitude, I'd like to get me a piece of it. I'm going to remind Brand tonight just how grateful he is that he met me.'

Ella had stayed out as long as public transport allowed but Aaron was nevertheless waiting for her when she got back, leaning against the library door.

No reprieve.

She'd three-quarters expected this, though, so she had a plan.

She would be *that* Ella—the cool, calm, un-

ouchable one—so he knew exactly what he'd get
f he pursued this insanity that she couldn't quite
oring herself to reject. With luck, he would run a
nile away from her, the way he'd run in Cambodia, and spare them both the heartache she feared
would be inevitable if they went down this path.

If not…well, they'd see.

'Are you going to wait up for me every night?'
she asked, in the amused tone that had infuriated
him in the past.

'I can wait in your bed if you prefer.'

The wind having effectively been taken out of
her sails, Ella headed slowly up the stairs without another word. Aaron followed her into her
room, reached for her.

'Wait,' she said, stepping back. 'You really
want to do this?'

'Yes.'

'One hundred per cent sure?'

'Yes.'

She sighed. 'It's going to end in tears, you
know.'

'I'll take my chances.'

Another sigh. 'Okay, then—but, first, ground
rules.'

He nodded, deadly serious.

'No PDAs,' she said. 'If this is casual sex, it stays in my bedroom—or your bedroom. No touchy-feely stuff beyond bed. And *absolutely* nothing in front of Tina or Brand or Kiri.'

'Agreed.'

'When one or the other of us decides the arrangement is over there will be no questions, no comments, no recriminations, no clinging. I will let you go as easily as that...' she clicked her fingers '...if you're the one ending things. And I expect you to do the same.'

He narrowed his eyes. 'Agreed.'

'No prying into my private life.'

He looked at her.

'Agreed?' she asked impatiently.

'I don't know what "prying" means to you—you're supersensitive about things other people consider normal conversation, and I don't want you taking a machete to my head if I ask what any reasonable person would think is an innocuous question.'

'If you think I'm unreasonable, why do you want to go down this path?'

He smiled, a smile that held the promise of hot, steamy sex. 'Oh, I think you know why, Ella.'

She was blushing again.

'What about if I agree that you are under no obligation to tell me anything that makes you uncomfortable?' he asked.

She digested that. 'Fair enough. Agreed. And ditto for you.'

'No need. You can ask me anything you want, and I'll answer you.'

That threw her, but she nodded. 'But I won't ask. Any conditions from your side?'

'One. Monogamy. Nobody else, while you're sleeping with me.'

'Agreed,' she said, but she tinkled out a little laugh to suggest she thought that was quaint. 'Anything else?'

'No. So take off your clothes.'

## CHAPTER ELEVEN

'I DO LIKE a masterful man,' Ella said. And then she reached for the hem of her dress.

But Aaron stopped her. 'I've changed my mind,' he said. 'Come here.'

Ella stepped towards him, her eyebrows raised in that practised, disdainful way that seemed to aggravate him.

When she reached him, he took the neckline of her cotton dress in his hands, and ripped the dress down the front.

A surprised 'Oh…' whooshed out of her. There went the practised disdain.

She looked up at him. His face was stark as he dragged her bra down her arms, imprisoning her with the straps, and bent his head to her breasts. He sucked one nipple, hard, into his mouth, and she gasped. Moved to the other. He eased back to look into her eyes as he pushed her tattered dress almost casually over her hips until it dropped to the floor. 'I'll buy you another,' he said.

She couldn't speak, couldn't raise her defensive shield of indifference. Could only wait and watch. Her arms were still trapped, and he made no move to free them. Instead, he brought his hands up to cup her breasts, thumbs smoothing across her nipples, and then lowered his mouth again.

How much time had passed—a minute? Ten? Longer? He wouldn't let her move, just kept up that steady pressure, hands and lips, until she was almost weeping with pleasure. Ella was desperate to touch him, but every time she tried to reach around to unhook her bra and free herself, he stymied her.

At last he stepped back, examined her with one long, lascivious look from her head to her toes. Then his hands went to the front of her panties and she felt, heard, the fine cotton tear. 'I'll replace those too,' he said softly, and then her breath shuddered out, rough and choppy, as one of his hands reached between her legs. Within moments she was shuddering as the pleasure tore through her like a monsoon. Hot, wet, wild.

He spun her, unhooking her bra with a swift efficiency that seemed to scorn his earlier languorous attention to her body. With the same speed, he stripped off his own clothes. Then his hands were on her again, arousing her, preparing her, as he backed the two of them towards the bed.

He fell onto the bed, on his back, and dragged her on top of him. 'Here, let me.' His voice was hoarse and urgent as he positioned her over him, moving her legs so that they fell on either side of his and thrusting blindly towards her centre.

'Wait,' she said.

It took only moments for her to raise herself, straddling him with her knees on each side of his straining body. She reached over him, grabbed a condom from the drawer. She ripped the package open with her teeth, slid the sheath onto him with slow, steady movements. Smoothing it as he jumped against her hand. And then she took him inside her with one undulating swirl of her hips. Stilled, keeping him there, not letting him move, deep inside her.

'No,' she said, as he started to buck upwards against her. 'Let me.' And, rising and falling in smooth, steady waves, she tightened herself around him until he gasped her name. Clutching her hips, he jammed her down on top of him and exploded.

Ella, following him into ecstasy, collapsed on top of him. She stayed there, spent, as his hands threaded through her hair, stroking and sliding.

She wanted to stay like that all night, with Aaron inside her, his hands in her hair, his mouth close enough to kiss.

Except that he hadn't kissed her. Not once.

For some reason, she didn't like that.

*It's just casual sex*, she reminded herself.

On that thought, she disengaged herself from his body and got off the bed. Pulling her hair back over her shoulders, she smiled serenely down at him. 'Excellent, thank you,' she said. 'But there's no need for you to stay. I'll see you tomorrow night.'

Tina had assorted chores to do the next day, so she left Kiri in Ella's sole company.

Ella had taken him to the park to practise catching the cricket ball. Was that the hardest, unkindest ball in international sport? Ella thought so, as she looked at her bruised shin.

So for the afternoon she'd chosen a more intellectual pursuit—painting. It was a challenge to keep Kiri's paint set in the vicinity of the special child-sized activity table Tina had moved into the library for him, but they'd accomplished it.

As assorted paintings, laid out across every available surface, were drying, she and Kiri curled up together in one of the massive leather chairs, where she entertained him by letting him play with her cellphone.

She was laughing at Kiri's attempt at an emoticon-only text message when Aaron walked in.

'Shouldn't you be on set?' she asked, sitting up straighter.

'I'm on a break so thought I'd come back to the house. What happened to your leg?'

'Cricket-ball injury. That's a sport I am never going to figure out.' She gestured around the room. 'Check out Kiri's paintings while you're here. Which one's for Dad, Kiri?'

Kiri scrambled out of the chair. 'Two of them. Here's Mum…' He was pointing out a painting of a black-haired woman in an orange dress. 'And here's Ella.' In her nursing uniform.

Ella felt her stomach drop with a heavy thud. Just what the man needed; his ex-wife and his current lover, as depicted by his son, who knew nothing of the tension in either relationship.

But Aaron was smiling like it was the most

wonderful gift in the world. 'Fabbo. One day, when you're famous, these are going to be worth a fortune.'

Kiri giggled, and then went to perch back with Ella. 'Ella's teaching me the phone,' he confided. 'I called Tina.'

'You're not international roaming, are you?' Aaron asked. 'That will cost you a fortune.'

Ella shrugged, not having the heart to deny Kiri. 'They're only short calls.' She smiled at Kiri as she scrolled through her contact list.

'See, Kiri, there's Dad's number. If you hit this, it will call him. Yes, perfect.'

Aaron's phone rang, and he dutifully answered it and had a moment's conversation with Kiri.

And then Aaron tossed metaphorical hands in the air. He asked Ella for her phone number, punched it into his contact list, then handed his phone to Kiri, showed him the entry and let him call her.

She and Kiri chatted for a while, as though they were on opposite sides of the world instead of sitting together.

Then Kiri looked pleadingly at his father. 'Dad, can I have a phone?'

Aaron laughed. 'Who do you need to call, mate?' he asked.

'You. Mum. Tina. Jenny. And Ella.'

'Well, calling Ella might be tricky,' Aaron explained, and lifted Kiri into his arms. 'Because we'll never know where in the world she is. And we don't want to wake her up at midnight!'

An excellent reminder, Ella thought, of the transience of their current arrangement—because at some point in the near future she would indeed be somewhere else in the world, far away from Aaron and Kiri.

When Aaron took his leave a short while later, she felt ill at ease.

It had been a strange interlude. Why had he even come? Maybe he didn't trust her with Kiri after all, and was checking up on her.

But it hadn't felt like that. In fact, he'd seemed delighted at her obviously close relationship with Kiri. And not at all freaked out at having a painting of her presented to him as a gift, which must have been awkward.

Knowing how much Aaron adored Kiri, and how keen he'd been to keep the two parts of this London life separate, well, it didn't make sense.

And Ella didn't like it.

* * *

Ella spent the next three days in a kind of hellish heaven.

Taking care of Kiri during the day and spending her nights with Aaron.

She adored her time with Kiri. She took him to Madame Tussaud's and to see the changing of the guard at Buckingham Palace, toy shopping for the baby, and for him. In the process, falling a little more in love with him every day.

She longed for her nights with Aaron. The pleasure that made her want to sigh and scream, the roughness and gentleness, the speed and languor, and everything in between.

But the arrangement was playing havoc with her emotions. Kiri's innocent stories about his father were making her feel altogether too soppy about a casual sex partner. And there were moments during the steamy nights when she and Aaron seemed to forget their agreed roles, becoming almost like real parents having the whole family chat.

Minus the kissing.

An omission that should have reassured her that this was just sex…but didn't.

And then, after five consecutive nights of lovemaking, Ella opened the morning paper and the sordidness of her current situation was thrown into sudden, sharp relief.

Only one half-column of words, not even a photo. But, still, the wreck of her life came crashing back.

It was an article about Javier, full of platitudes from various authorities with no actual news of his fate. But it felt like an omen, and it savaged Ella's conscience. Because she realised that since being with Aaron, not only had she been free of nightmares but she hadn't had any thoughts about Javier either.

So when Aaron came to her room that night, carrying a bag, she pleaded a migraine, knowing she looked ill enough for him to believe her.

'Can I get you anything?' he asked, concern creasing his forehead as he dumped the bag carelessly on her bed.

She forced a strained smile. 'Hey, I'm a nurse, remember?'

He nodded, and then completely disarmed her by drawing her against him and just holding her. 'Sleep well, angel,' he said, and left her.

*Angel?*

That was going to have to be nipped in the bud.

She approached the bag with some trepidation. Pulled out a raspberry-coloured dress that even she could see was something special, and a bra and panties set in a matching shade that was really too beautiful to wear. The replacements for the things Aaron had ripped off her, obviously—although, strictly speaking, he didn't owe her a bra.

She stared at them, spread on the bed, and tried to shrug off the sense of doom that gripped her.

Aaron was dragged out of a deep slumber by a kind of screeching wail, abruptly cut off.

He sat up, perfectly still, perfectly silent, and listened.

Nothing.

He shook his head to clear it.

Nothing. Imagination.

So—back to sleep. He gave his pillow a thump and lay back down.

Sat back up. Nope—something was wrong. He could feel it.

He got out of bed, padded out of the room, shirtless and in his shorts.

He opened the door to Kiri's room opposite and peered in. He was sleeping soundly.

So…Ella? He opened the door to her room quietly.

She was lying perfectly still, her eyes wide and staring, her hands jammed against her mouth.

He didn't think. Just slid into bed beside her, took her in his arms and arranged her limbs for maximum sleeping comfort.

She said nothing, but she didn't kick him away, which had to be a good sign.

'Just to be clear,' he said, 'I'm not asking questions. So don't even think of telling me to leave.'

She looked at him for one heartbeat, two, three. Then she closed her eyes, and eventually he felt her ease into sleep.

It wasn't going to be easy to not ask at some point. He'd better wear his thermal underwear to ward off the frostbite during that moment. Hmm. Oddly enough, it didn't daunt him. He snuggled her a little closer, kissed the top of her head. *One day, Ella, I'll know it all.*

Damn Aaron James.

It was his fault she was in a dingy hotel room that wasn't big enough to swing a rodent in, let alone a cat.

Not that she hadn't slept in an array of sub-

standard places over the years, though none had
ever cost her a staggering hundred and twenty
pounds per night.

He'd had to come into her room last night when
she'd been at her most vulnerable. And sneaked
out this morning without waking her, without
having the decency to talk about it so she could
slap him down.

So here she was. Hiding out. Staying away until
she could find the best way to end things with
him. Because things were just not quite casual
enough to make this arrangement work.

Aaron was moving house tomorrow. That
should signal the end of their liaison. She
shouldn't have let Aaron persuade her in the first
place. Because look where it had landed her. She
was confused about Aaron, guilt-stricken about
Javier, miserable about everything—and in a
shoebox-sized room that was costing her a bomb.

Ella sighed heavily, and sat dispiritedly on the
bed. It was kind of slippery, as if the mattress
protector was plastic. She popped into the bathroom to splash some water on her face and the
*eau de* public toilet aroma jammed into her nostrils.

Well, that settled one thing: she might have to

sleep here, but she wasn't going to breathe in that smell until she had to. She was going out for the evening.

In fact, for this one night she was going to rediscover the excesses she'd left behind in Cambodia. And when she was sozzled enough, she would return to face the room.

She would *not* run headlong to Tina's and one last night with Aaron.

Which was how Ella found herself playing pool with Harry, Neal and Jerome; three gorgeous, safely gay guys.

She was hot. Sweaty. Dishevelled. A little bit drunk.

Just how you wanted to look for a surprise visit from your lover.

Because that was definitely Aaron James, entering the pub just as she hit the white ball so awkwardly it jumped off the table.

Aaron James, who was standing there, glaring at her.

Fate. It really wasn't working for her.

# CHAPTER TWELVE

HE'D BEEN WORKING his way through the pubs in the vicinity of Tina and Brand's because he'd known Ella wasn't staying with friends, as she'd told Tina, and he suspected she wouldn't stray too far, given Tina's advanced pregnancy. So it wasn't exactly fate that he'd found her, because this was the seventh pub he'd tried. But it sure felt like it.

He should go, leave her to it. She didn't *have* to see him every night. Didn't have to get his permission to stay out all night. Didn't have to explain why she was laughing over a pool table with three handsome men.

Except that she kind of *did* have to.

And it would have been stupid to search through the pubs of Mayfair for her and then turn tail the moment he found her.

She was wearing a skin-tight black skirt that would give a corpse a wet dream. A clingy silver singlet top just covering those perfect breasts.

Black high heels—that was a first, and a very sexy one. Her hair was piled on her head, who knew how it was staying up there? In fact, not all of it was. Her messy hair made him think of having her in bed.

Aaron watched as she bounced the white ball off the table. As all four of them chortled. He seethed as the blond guy kissed her. Felt murderous as the other two hugged her, one each side.

She knew he was here. He'd seen the flare in her eyes, the infinitesimal toss of her head as she'd directed her eyes away.

*Oh no you don't, Ella. Oh, no. You. Don't.*

Ella decided the best thing to do was carry on with her evening as though she hadn't seen Aaron standing on the other side of the pub with his hands fisted at his sides like he was trying not to punch something. She was not going to be made to feel guilty about this.

The guys started hunting in their pockets for beer money. Ella dug into her handbag. 'Don't think so,' she said mournfully, as she scrabbled around inside. And then her eyes widened. 'Hang on,' she said, and triumphantly drew a ten-pound note from the depths, along with one old mint and a paper clip.

'Hooray!' Jerome exclaimed with great enthusiasm. 'Off you go, my girl—to the bar.'

'Or maybe not.'

The voice came from behind Ella but she knew to whom it belonged. That accent.

She'd known he would come to her. Had expected it. Was she happy about it? Yes, unbelievably, given she'd intended to avoid him tonight, she was happy. *A bad sign.*

She looked over her shoulder at him. 'Hello, Aaron.'

'You and pool tables, what's up with that?' Aaron asked mildly. He tucked a strand of loose hair behind one of Ella's ears. 'Run out of money, sweetheart?'

'Yes,' she said, looking at him carefully as she turned fully towards him. He wasn't giving off *sweetheart* vibes. Aaron dug into his jeans pocket, pulled out a fifty-pound note and handed it to her.

'Are you going to introduce me to your friends?' he asked, as she stared at the cash as though she couldn't believe she was holding it.

'Huh?' she said eloquently.

'Your friends?' he prompted.

Ella looked around as though she'd forgotten their existence. Pulled herself together as she noted her three new drinking buddies gazing at her with avid interest.

'Oh. Yes,' she said, and hastily performed the introductions.

'And do you really want another drink, or shall we hand that money over to the guys and head off?'

Ella was torn.

'Ella? Are we staying or going?' Aaron asked, steel in his voice.

She *should* tell him to go to hell. But she found she didn't want to fight with Aaron. Not here. Didn't want to fight with him, period.

'I guess we're going,' she said. 'So here you go, boys, thanks for buying my drinks all night and I hope this covers it.' She smiled at them. 'I had a brilliant time. And remember what I said about LA. If you're ever there…'

Assorted hugs and kisses later, Ella did her slow walk out of the pub.

'You're not fooling me with the slow walk, Ella,' Aaron said as they reached the footpath.

She stopped. Turned to him. 'I don't know what you m—'

He pulled her into his arms sharply, shocking that sentence right out of her head.

He moved to kiss her but Ella put her hands up, pushing against his chest. 'You don't kiss me any more.'

'Is that so?' Aaron asked. Purely rhetorical—she had no time to answer as he planted his mouth on hers like a heat-seeking missile hitting its target. His hands went to her bottom and he pulled her against him, pelvis to pelvis.

Ella gasped as he released her, and her fingers came up to touch her mouth. 'Why are you so angry with me?'

Aaron looked down at her, unapologetic. 'Because you left me.'

Ella couldn't help herself—she touched his cheek.

She went to pull her hand away but Aaron caught it, held it against his face. 'And because I'm jealous,' he said.

'Jealous?'

Aaron nodded towards the pub.

Ella was stunned. 'But they're gay.'

He didn't miss a beat. 'I don't care if they're

eunuchs. Because it's not sex I'm talking about. We're monogamous, you and I, and I trust you with that.'

That certainty shook her. She swallowed hard. 'Then what?'

'It's the whole deal. Being with you. In the moment. In public. *That* smile. That's what I'm talking about.'

*That smile? Huh?* 'We're in the moment in public now,' she said. 'Which I hope you don't regret.' She tilted her head towards a small group of women as she tugged her hand free. They were staring at Aaron as they walked past. 'I think they know you. I keep forgetting you're a celebrity.'

'I don't care.'

'You're *supposed* to care. Just sex, on the quiet—no scandal. Look, let's be honest. It's not working out, this casual sex thing.'

'No, it's not.'

She couldn't think straight for a moment. Because he'd agreed with her. Which meant it was over. Just what she'd wanted.

'Right,' she said. And then, because she still couldn't think straight, 'Right.'

'We're going to have to renegotiate.'

'There doesn't seem to be much point to that, or much to negotiate *with*,' Ella said, as her brain finally engaged. 'Given you're moving out tomorrow, let's just call it quits.'

Aaron pursed his lips. 'Um—no.'

'No?'

'No.'

'Remember our agreement? No questions, no—'

'I don't give a toss about our agreement. We are not going to go our separate ways because you decided to click your fingers on a public street.'

'See? I told you it's not working. The casual sex deal meant no messy endings. And you're making it messy.'

'But it's not casual, is it, Ella? And I don't want to let you go.'

Her heart did that stuttering thing. She forced herself to ignore it. 'You knew there couldn't be anything except sex. And it will be too hard to keep even that going once we're living in different places.' Swallow. 'And I—I have an extra complication.'

'Which is?' he asked flatly.

'I have—I have…someone.'

'Look at me, Ella.'

She faced him squarely, threw back her head, eyes glittering with defiance.

'No, you don't,' Aaron said.

'Oh, for goodness' sake, I do! I do, I do!'

'If you had someone, you couldn't be with me the way you have been.'

She gasped. He couldn't have hurt her more if he'd stabbed her.

Because he was right.

How could she love Javier if she could pour herself into sex with Aaron in the no-holds-barred way that had become their signature? It had never happened before—only drunken fumbling that she'd run away from every single time. The antithesis of what she did with Aaron.

Aaron was looking at her with almost savage intensity. 'We need to settle this, and not here. Come with me.'

'Where are we going?'

'I don't know—a hotel.'

She laughed, but there was no softness in it. 'I have a hotel room. It stinks like a public toilet and has a plastic mattress protector. That sounds about right. Let's go there. And don't flinch like that.'

'I think we can do better than that, Ella.'

Ella wanted to scream. But she also wanted to cry. And instead of doing either, she was goading him, making everything ugly and tawdry, turning it into the one-night stand it should have always been. 'All right, then. Let's "settle" this,' she said. 'One last time. I'm up for it. You can use my body any way you want, and I will show you there is nothing romantic about an orgasm—it's just technique.'

'Is that so?'

'Let's find out. But if I'm going to play the mistress, I warn you now that I'm going to want access to the mini-bar.'

'Any way I can get you, Ella,' he said, unperturbed. 'You can devour everything in the mini-bar, order everything off the room-service menu, steal the fluffy robe, take the towels—anything you want.'

'I've always wanted to steal the fluffy robe,' Ella said, and took his arm.

# CHAPTER THIRTEEN

AARON HAILED A cab and asked to be taken to the closest five-star hotel. On the way, he called to check on Kiri and let Jenny, who'd arrived in the early evening, know he wouldn't be home that night.

Ella waited through the call, clearly still furious with him. Well, too damned bad.

Aaron hastily secured them a room for the night and as they headed for the hotel elevator, he drew Ella close to him, holding her rigid hand. He breathed in the slightly stale pub scent of her. But he couldn't have cared less whether she came to him straight from the shower or after running a marathon through the city sewers.

The elevator doors opened and then they were inside. Alone. The second the doors closed, he was kissing her, sliding his hands under her top. One hand moved up to cover her breast, moulding it to his palm, teasing the nipple to maddening hardness with unsteady fingers. He'd thought she might push him away but, no, she kissed him back, straining against him. He broke the kiss, his breath coming fast and hard now, and bent his mouth to her shoulder, biting her there.

The elevator stopped and they broke apart, staring at each other. Without a word, Aaron grabbed her hand and pulled her quickly out and along the corridor. His hands were shaking so much he almost couldn't work the door mechanism to their suite. And then they were inside and Aaron reached for her again. Wordless. Driven. Desperate.

But so was Ella.

She yanked his T-shirt up his chest and over his head. 'Ah,' she breathed, as her hands went to his hips and she pulled him toward her. She put her mouth on one of his nipples and held tight to his hips as he bucked against her.

'Ella,' he groaned, hands moving restlessly to try to hold onto her as her tongue flicked out. 'Let me touch you.'

'Not yet,' she said, and moved her mouth to his other nipple. As she did so, she started to undo the button fly of his jeans.

He groaned again but couldn't speak as her hands slid inside his underwear.

'Do you like me to touch you like this?' she asked.

'You know I— Ahh, Ella, you're killing me.'

Laughing throatily, Ella stepped back, started to undress.

'Hurry up,' she said, as he stood watching as she wriggled out of her skirt.

It was all the encouragement Aaron needed. In record time, he'd stripped.

Ella, naked except for her high heels, turned to drape her clothes over the back of a handily positioned chair. Aaron came up behind her and caught her against his chest. His arms circled her, hands reaching for her breasts.

She dropped her clothes and leaned back against him, thrusting her breasts into his hands. She moaned as he kissed the side of her neck, gasped as one questing hand dived between her thighs.

'Oh, you're good at this,' Ella said, as she felt her orgasm start to build.

'You can still talk,' Aaron said against her ear. 'So not good enough.'

With that, he bent her forward at the waist until she was clinging to the chair, and thrust inside her. His hands were on her hips as he continued o move inside her, pulling all the way out after each thrust before slamming into her again.

The feel of her bottom against him, the intoxicating sounds of her pleasure as she orgasmed, clenching around him until he thought he'd faint from desire, the exquisite friction of his movements in and out of her built together until the blood was roaring in his head and demanding he take her harder, harder, harder.

Ella. This was Ella.

His.

Ella slumped against Aaron. After that explosive orgasm, he'd turned her around to face him, kissed her for the longest time, and now he was holding her with every bit of gentleness his lovemaking had lacked.

What she'd meant to do was give him a clinical experience. Instead, she'd drenched herself in soul-deep, emotionally fraught lust. Her anger was gone. And the bitterness. She felt purged, almost. Which wasn't the way it was supposed to be.

Nothing had changed. Nothing that could open the way for her to have what she wanted with a clear conscience. Sex couldn't cure things. Even phenomenal sex. Life couldn't be that simple.

Javier was still out there, the uncertainty of his fate tying her to him. Aaron still had a problematic ex-wife and a little boy whose inevitable loss, when they went their separate ways, would devastate her.

'Did I hurt you?' he asked, kissing the top of her head.

'This really is a regular post-coital question of yours, isn't it?'

'No. It's just that I've only ever lost control with you.'

There was a lump in her throat. 'Well, stop asking,' she said, when she trusted herself to speak. 'You didn't hurt me.' *Not in that way.*

'I didn't even think about a condom,' Aaron said.

Ella shrugged restlessly, eased out of his arms. 'I know. I wasn't thinking straight either. And me a nurse.'

'I'm sorry.'

'Me too, but it's done. Not that it's really the point, but I'm on the Pill. So if that worries you, at least—'

'No. No—I'm not worried about that. At least,

not for myself. I wish I *could* have a child with you, Ella. Not to replace Sann but for you.'

That lump was in her throat again. She turned away. 'Complicating as all hell, though, pregnancy, for casual sex partners,' she said, trying for light and airy and not quite making it. She remembered ordering him to never say Sann's name again. But it didn't hurt to hear the name now. Not from him.

Aaron—what an unlikely confidant. The only one who knew her pain.

She cleared her throat, 'But now, do you think we could actually move out of this hallway? And where are those fluffy robes?'

Aaron obligingly guided Ella into the lounge area of the suite. He fetched a robe for each of them, and watched as Ella belted hers on, then sat on the sofa to remove her shoes.

He came to sit beside her, slipped an arm around her shoulders and drew her back against him so that her head was against his shoulder.

'You know, don't you, that I'm not a nice person?' she said.

'No, I don't know that. I've watched you work. Seen how much you care. The way you are with Kiri. I know how protective you are of your family. I know you wanted to adopt an orphan from Cambodia, and I've seen what the grief of that did to you. These things don't add up to "not nice".'

'I've been jealous of my sister, of the baby. That's not nice.'

'It doesn't look to me like Tina's had her eyes scratched out,' Aaron said calmly.

'Well, I'm over it now,' she admitted. 'But it took some soul searching.'

'I'm thinking soul searching is a bit of a hobby of yours.'

'And I— Over the past year I've done things. Things I'm not proud of.'

'You've had a lot to deal with. Cut yourself some slack, Ella.'

'You stopped kissing me.'

'And you think that was some kind of judgement?' He broke off, laughed softly. 'That was a defence mechanism. That's all.'

'What?'

'Casual sex? Just sex—no kissing, because kissing is not casual.'

'Oh.'

They stayed sitting in silence, his arm around her, for a long moment.

*Now what?* Ella wondered.

But then Aaron broke the silence. 'So tell me, Ella, about the "someone". The someone I know you don't have. The someone I think you once *had*. Past tense. Right?'

'Had *and* have.'

'Hmm, I'm going to need a little more.'

'His name is Javier. He's a doctor. Spanish. He was kidnapped in Somalia.' *Whew.* 'There was an article in the paper this morning.' She looked up at him briefly. 'Hence my need to go a little off the rails tonight.'

Aaron nodded, saying nothing. And somehow it was easy to relax against him and continue. Aaron, her confidant. 'We were in love. Very newly in love, so new that nobody else knew about it, which was a blessing the way things turned out, because I couldn't have borne the questions, the sympathy.' Pause. 'I should have been with him that day. It was my twenty-fifth birthday, two years ago. I was supposed to be in the jeep with him.'

Long pause. She could almost hear her own pulse. 'You've got no idea how awful it was. The conditions. The soul-sapping struggle to provide healthcare to people who desperately needed it.

Because even before you think about treating illnesses like malaria and TB and pneumonia and HIV, you know that the drought, the violence, the poverty, the poor harvests have made malnutrition a force that simply can't be reckoned with. The kids are starving. Sometimes walking hundreds of kilometres just to drop dead in front of you. And ten thousand people a day are dying.

'And your colleagues are being kidnapped or even murdered, and armed opposition groups make it almost impossible to reach people in need, even though everyone *knows* the suffering, and even hiring a vehicle to get to people is a tense negotiation with clans in constant conflict, and the very people who are providing the tiny bit of security you can get are okay with the deaths and the kidnappings.'

She stopped again. 'Sorry I'm so emotional.' She shook her head. 'No, I'm not sorry. It needs emotion. When you're resuscitating a one-year-old girl, and there is a tiny boy next to her so frail that only a stethoscope over his heart tells you he's alive, and two more critically ill children are waiting behind you, why *not* get emotional?'

His hand was in her hair, stroking, soothing. 'Go on, Ella. I'm here.'

'Anyway. Javier and I were heading to one of the refugee camps in Kenya. But I got malaria and I couldn't go. So I'm here and he's somewhere. Alive, dead, injured, safe? I don't know.' Ella drew in a shuddering breath. 'And I feel guilty, about having a normal life while he's lost. And guilty that I can be with you like this when I should be waiting for him. And just plain guilty. I'm a wreck.'

'Ah, Ella.' He eased her out from under his arm and turned her to face him. 'I'd tell you it's not your fault, that you have a right to go on with your life, that anyone who loved you would want that for you, that you wouldn't want Javier to be trapped in the past if your situations were reversed; but that's not going to set you free, is it?' He ran his fingers down her cheek. 'You have to be ready to let it go.'

'The thing is I don't know what he'd want me to do, or what he'd do in my place.'

'That says something, doesn't it? You were only twenty-five, and in a very new relationship. If you're really going to keep a candle burning in the window for the rest of your life, I'm going to have to find the guy and make sure he's worth it, and I don't really want to do that. Somalia is scary!'

Ella smiled. 'You really do have that heroic thing going on, don't you? I think you *would* go there if you thought it would help me.'

'Nah. It's not heroic, it's self-interest. Memories can bring on rose-tinted-glasses syndrome. Which, in this case, makes it really hard for a mere actor to measure up to a Spanish doctor kidnapped while saving lives in Africa. Even with the malaria documentary under my belt, I'm coming in a poor second.' He kissed her forehead. 'But it's just possible, in a real flesh-and-blood contest, I could edge past him. Unless he happens to be devastatingly attractive as well.'

'As a matter of fact...' Ella trailed off with a laugh.

'Well, that sucks. Maybe I *won't* go and find him after all.'

'Yeah, well, Somalia really *is* scary, so I wouldn't let you go. I wouldn't like to lose you too.' Ella resettled her head on his shoulder. 'Okay—now you know all the salient bits about my past. So, let's talk about you. You said I could ask you anything, and you'd answer.'

'Ask away.'

'I'll start with something easy. Tina told me you raised your sisters after your parents died.'

'Easy? Ha! It was like a brother-sister version of *The Taming of the Shrew*, but in triplicate.'

Ella smiled. 'And you love them very much.'

'Oh, yes. Lucinda, Gabriella and Nicola. My parents were killed in a boating accident when I was eighteen. The girls were fifteen, twelve and ten. I was old enough to look after them, so I did. End of story, really. Two of them are married with kids now, one is married to her job—she's an actuary but she looks like a fashion designer—and all of them are happy.'

'It can't have been easy.'

'We had some nail-biting moments over the years, no doubt about it. But I won't go into the scary boyfriend stories or the fights over schoolwork and curfews. We just belonged together. Simple.'

Pause. And then, 'Is it okay to ask about Rebecca? Like, how you met?'

'Sure. I met her through Brand. The way I meet all my women.'

Ella pinched his thigh.

'All right, not *all* of them,' he amended, laughing. 'Let me give you the abridged version. We met at one of Brand's parties. He was living in Los Angeles back then and I was over there, trying to make the big time—unsuccessfully. Rebecca was doing the same, equally unsuccessfully.'

'So you drowned your sorrows together?'

'Something like that. We were an item in pretty short order. Happily ever after. For a while at least.'

'What went wrong?'

'Nothing. That's what I thought, anyway.' He sighed. 'But looking back, it was all about work. When we returned to Australia I started getting steady jobs. We adopted Kiri and everything seemed fine. But I got more work. Better work. And more work. Making a fortune, no worries. But Rebecca's career stalled. She wasn't happy, and I was too busy to notice. Until it was too late. She started doing a few outrageous things to get publicity in the mistaken belief it would help things along. And before I knew it, it was party, party, party. Drugs. Booze. More drugs. I know Tina told you about the rehab. Well, Rebecca's been to rehab before. Twice.' He shrugged. 'I'm praying this time it will work. This place, it's called Trust, it really seems good.'

'Oh, Trust—I know it, and it is good. She's in safe hands there.'

'Thanks, Ella.'

Ella brought his hand to her lips and kissed it. 'So I guess you've been trying to make up for being too busy to notice when things started to go wrong.'

'That's about the sum of it.'

'Am I going to do the "not your fault" routine?'

Aaron touched her hair. 'No. I'm as bad as you are when it comes to guilt, I think.'

'And Kiri? Why adopt? And why do you have full custody?'

'The adoption? We'd always planned to adopt a child in need and that just happened to come before trying for our own. The custody thing? Well, no matter what's between Rebecca and me, she wants only the best for Kiri, and she recognised that that was living with me, because although she likes to pretend she's in control, she knows she's not.'

She touched his hand. 'You love her. Rebecca.'

'Yes, I do,' Aaron said. 'But it's no longer *that* love. I care about her, as a friend and as the mother of my son.'

'It sounds very mature.'

'Hmm, well, don't be thinking it's all sugar plums and fairy cakes, far from it. She likes to get what she wants.' He laughed. 'I suppose we all do, if it comes to that. But when she needs something, she tends to forget we're divorced and she's not above a bit of manipulation. That can make it hard for us to move on.'

'She wouldn't like it? The fact that I'm here with you.'

'Probably not,' he admitted. 'Unless she had someone first.'

'So you won't tell her.'

'That depends, Ella. On whether we're sticking to our initial arrangement.'

Silence.

Ella wasn't ready to face that.

She got to her feet, headed for the mini-bar and started looking through the contents. 'So,' she said, moving various bottles around without any real interest, 'getting back to the important stuff. Condoms. Or the lack of them. Pregnancy we've covered. But I can also reassure you that I was checked before I left Cambodia and am disease-free. It's something I do regularly, because of my work with AIDS patients.'

'Me too, disease-free, I mean. I've been an avid fan of the condom for a long, long time.'

She turned. 'But weren't you and Rebecca starting to try for...?'

'Trying for a baby? No. For the last year we weren't trying *anything*. You see, along with the drugs came other problems—new experiences Rebecca wanted, such as sex with a variety of men. Including two of my friends. *Ex*-friends,' he clarified. 'I could forgive her for that. I *did* forgive her, knowing what was going on with her. But I couldn't...well, I just couldn't after that.'

'I don't know what to say to that.'

'Not much *to* say. I did try to keep my marriage together, because commitments are important to me. But some things just...change.'

Ella thought about that. What a lovely thing to accept. *Some things just change.*

'Anyway, enough gloom.' He walked over to her, gave her a quick, hard kiss. 'Come and have a bath with me.'

Aaron grabbed the scented crystals beside the deep bath and threw them in as the tub filled. Then he lifted her in his arms and kissed her as he stepped into the water, settled. Kept kissing her until the bath was full. He took the soap from her and washed her, kissing, touching, until she was gasping for air. But he wouldn't take her. Not this time. 'Condoms, so you don't have to wonder,' he said, by way of explanation.

'I have some in my bag,' she said, shivering with desire.

'Monogamy, remember?' Aaron said. 'I don't think roaming around London with a bag full of condoms fits the principle.'

'Just handbag history—like the expired bus tickets in there. I wasn't going to use them.'

'It's okay, Ella. I know that. Somehow, I really do know that.' He got to his feet, streaming water, but before he could leave the tub Ella got to her knees. 'Not yet,' she said, and looked up at him as she took him in her mouth.

The next morning Aaron ordered a veritable banquet for breakfast.

He was whistling as he opened the door, as the food was laid out in the living room. The robe he'd purchased for Ella was in its neat drawstring bag, positioned on one of the chairs.

He'd left Ella in bed with the television remote control, and was halfway to the bedroom to fetch her for their lovers' feast, mid-whistle, when he heard it. A sound between a choke and a gasp.

'Ella, what is it?' he asked, hurrying into the room.

She was pale. Deathly so. Like the life had drained out of her. She looked up at him, and then, like she couldn't help herself, back at the television.

There was a man being interviewed. A gaunt man. Beautiful—not handsome, beautiful.

'It's him,' Ella said.

# CHAPTER FOURTEEN

'HIM?' AARON ASKED. But he knew.

The news moved onto the next item and it was like a signal had been transmitted directly to Ella's brain.

She got out of bed. 'I have to go,' she said. But then she simply stood there, shivering.

'Go where?'

'Africa.'

'You can't go anywhere in that state, and certainly not Africa.'

'Don't tell me what to do,' she said, and started dressing. It took her less than a minute.

'Ella, you have to talk to me.'

'I did enough talking last night.'

'For God's sake Ella, I—'

'No,' she cried, and then raced to her bag. She looked up, wild-eyed. 'Money. I don't have money for a cab.'

'Calm down, Ella. I'll take you where you need to go.'

'I don't want you to take me anywhere. I want—I want—' She stopped, looked at him, then burst into tears.

Aaron tried to take her in his arms but she wrenched away from him, turned aside to hide her face and walked to the window. She cried as she looked out at the world. Cried as though her soul was shattering.

And just watching her, helpless, Aaron felt his life start to disintegrate.

Gradually, her sobs subsided. She stood leaning her forehead against the window.

Aaron came up behind her, touched her gently on the shoulder. She stiffened but didn't pull away.

'You're going to him,' he said.

'Of course.'

'You're still in love with him, then.'

Pause. And then, 'I have to be. And I have to go.' She turned to face him. 'I know I already owe you money but will you lend me enough for a cab?'

'You don't owe me anything, Ella.'

Aaron grabbed her by her upper arms and drew her forward. 'I'll wait for you to sort this out, Ella. I'll be here, waiting.'

'I don't deserve for anyone to wait for me,' she said, and her voice was colourless. 'Because *I* didn't wait. I *should* have been waiting for him. I *intended* to wait for him. But I didn't. Instead I—I was…' A breath shuddered in. Out. 'I can't stand it. I have to go. Now. I have to go.'

'All right.' Aaron grabbed his jeans and pulled out a handful of notes. 'Take this. And here…' He grabbed the hotel notepad and pen from beside the phone and scribbled a few lines. 'It's my address in London. We'll be there from today. And this…' he dashed another line on the paper '…is the phone number for the house. You've already got my mobile number. Whatever you need, Ella, whenever.'

'Thank you,' Ella said, and raced from the room without another word or glance.

Aaron looked at the sumptuous breakfast, at the robe he'd bought for Ella just because she'd joked about wanting to steal one. She hadn't seen it, wouldn't have taken it if she had.

Javier was back. And that was that.

And then, two days later, Rebecca disappeared from rehab in the company of a fellow addict, a film producer, and he knew he was going to have to fly to LA at some point to bail her out of some heinous situation.

Yep. That really was that.

Ella felt weird, being with Javier, even after a week together.

He was the same and yet not the same.

Every time she broached the subject of the past two years he closed the discussion down. He simply thought they would pick up exactly where they'd left off, as though those two years had never happened, but Ella couldn't get her head into the same space.

She couldn't bear to sleep with him, for one thing.

She told *him* it was to give them a chance to get to know each other again. She told *herself* it was because she'd been stupid enough to forget the condom with Aaron—that meant she had to wait and see, because things *did* go wrong with the Pill.

But, really, she just didn't want to.

She tried, desperately, to remember what it had been like, that one time with Javier, but the only images that formed were of Aaron.

So it would have been disloyal somehow. To

Javier, who didn't deserve for her to be thinking about another man. And, bizarrely, to Aaron, who was now effectively out of her life.

Ella sighed and got out of bed in her tiny hotel room. Padded into the bathroom and looked in the cabinet mirror. What did Aaron see that made him fall on her like he was starving for the taste of her? She was beautiful, she'd been told that often enough to believe it, but had never thought it important. Until now. Because maybe Aaron wouldn't have wanted her so much if she'd looked different.

Was it shallow to be glad that something as in-significant as the shape of her mouth made Aaron kiss her as though it was the only thing in the world he needed?

Ella gave herself a mental shake. She had to stop thinking about Aaron. Javier was her future. Javier, who'd been returned to her, like a miracle.

Today, they would fly to London so she could introduce Javier to Tina, who'd had the Javier story thrown at her like a dart as Ella had packed her bags. He would be there with her for the baby's birth. Even her parents would be com-ing in a month, to meet their grandchild…and the strange man who'd been kept a secret from them. And wouldn't *that* be interesting, after her mother's blistering phone soliloquy on the subject of Ella keeping her in the dark?

Out of control, the whole thing. A runaway train, speeding her into an alien future.

Ella closed her eyes.

*Did I hurt you?* Aaron's voice whispered through her memory.

*Yes*, she answered silently. *Yes, you did.*


Heathrow was bedlam, but Ella almost dreaded exiting the airport.

She was so nervous.

About introducing Javier to Tina and Brand.

And about the inevitable meeting between Javier and Aaron.

Javier, she'd discovered, was the jealous type. Not the cute, huggable kind of jealous Aaron had been that night outside the pub in Mayfair. Sort of *scary* jealous. The prospect of him and Aaron in the same room was enough to make her break into a cold sweat.

She welcomed the flash of cameras as they emerged from Customs. Javier was whisked away for a quick photo op, and she was glad. It meant she would have a moment to herself.

Or not.

Because, groan-inducingly, Aaron was there, waiting for her. In his T-shirt and jeans. Looking desperately unhappy.

He strode forward. 'Tina sent me instead of a limo. Sorry. I tried to get out of it, but nobody's allowed to say no to her at the moment, she's been so worried about you.'

'Everyone must hate me.'

'Nobody hates you, Ella. Everyone just wants things to work out.'

Ella could feel one of those awful blushes racing up her neck. 'I'm sorry. For running out like that, I mean. I should have explained, I should have—'

'Ella, don't. I know you. I know what you went through. I know why you had to go. I should have just stood aside. Please don't cry.'

Ella blinked hard, managed to gain her composure. 'You always seem to know. I wish... Oh, he's coming.'

Javier, unsmiling, put his arm around Ella the moment he reached them.

Aaron held out his hand, just as unsmiling.

*It was like an old cowboy movie, trigger fingers at the ready*, Ella thought, a little hysterically.

'Javier,' Aaron said. His hand was still out, ignored.

Ella took Javier's elbow. 'Javier, this is a friend of Tina and Brand's. And mine. Aaron James. He's very kindly giving us a ride.' Ugh, was that a *wheedle* in her voice? Disgusting.

'I'm pleased to meet you,' Javier said solemnly, at last taking Aaron's proffered hand for a single jerking shake.

Aaron gave him a narrow-eyed look. There was a small uncomfortable pause and then, taking their baggage cart, Aaron said, 'Follow me.'

Javier held Ella back for a moment. 'I don't like the way he looks at you,' he said.

Ella gritted her teeth. This was the fifth time in a week Javier had taken exception to the way a man had looked at her. She would have loved to tell him to get over it, but this particular time he had a right to be suspicious.

Aaron looked over his shoulder, no doubt wondering what was keeping them.

Looking straight ahead, Ella took Javier's arm and followed Aaron.

It was always going to be an uncomfortable drive, but this was ridiculous.

Aaron was fuming, relegated to the role of chauffer.

Javier spoke only to Ella, and only in Spanish. Charming!

Ella answered him in English, but the agonised looks he was catching in the rear-view mirror told Aaron she knew her Spaniard was behaving like a jackass.

Okay—so maybe jackass was his word, not Ella's, but he stood by it. *Nice choice, Ella.*

It was a relief to pull up at the house. After he helped hoist their luggage out of the boot, Aaron drew Ella a little aside. 'Ella, so you know, Tina's insisting I come to dinner tonight,' he said softly.

'That…that's fine,' Ella said, glancing nervously at Javier, who was giving her a very dark look as he picked up their bags. With a poor attempt at a smile Ella hurried back to Javier, took his arm and ushered him quickly into the house.

Aaron sighed, wondered why he'd even bothered warning her about him being at dinner. However prepared any of them were, when you parcelled it all up—Ella's uncharacteristically submissive demeanour, Javier's haughty unfriendliness, the prospect of witnessing the reunited lovebirds cooing at each other all evening, and his own desire to do some kind of violence to Javier that would ruin at least one perfect cheekbone—dinner was going to be a fiasco of epic proportions.

Aaron had been braced ever since he'd got to Tina's, but he still couldn't help the way his eyes darted to the door of the living room when it opened for the final two guests.

Ella looked like a deer caught in the headlights. She was wearing a dress. Dark grey. Silky. Simple. Classy. She was wearing her black high heels. He wanted to run his hands up her legs. He could drool at any moment.

Their eyes met for one sharp, tense moment and she blushed.

Javier said something and Aaron shifted his gaze.

Javier was everything Aaron wasn't. It was more pronounced tonight than it had been at the airport. Javier was elegant and sophisticated. Stylish in that way Europeans seemed to manage so effortlessly. Javier's hair was jet black, lying against his perfect skull in well-behaved waves. His eyes were equally black—dramatically moody. He was dressed in black pants and a pale pinkish-purple shirt that not many men could carry off.

And since when had Aaron ever noticed, let alone cared about, what other men were wearing?

He tore his eyes away, took a bracing sip of his Scotch.

Hellos were said. A drink pressed into Javier's hand, another into Ella's. Tina kissed Javier on the cheek. Javier touched Tina's ringlets as though entranced.

Tina laughed. 'A curse, this hair. Only Brand likes it.'

Javier smiled. 'Not only Brand. I like it too. Lively hair.'

Tina laughed again, shaking her head until her curls danced a little.

Great, Aaron thought. Javier was going to be adored by Ella's sister. Just great.

Brand, who was standing beside him, made a disgusted sound and rolled his eyes. He'd always known Brand was an excellent judge of character.

Tina was saying something about the need to fatten Ella up.

'It's her work,' Javier said, pulling Ella very close. 'She worked too hard in Cambodia.'

'Getting any information out of Ella about her

work is like pulling teeth, but Aaron told us a little about the conditions there.'

Javier looked straight at Aaron. Hostile.

Not that he could work out the whole backstory of Aaron's obsession with Ella from one glancing look.

Could he?

'And what were *you* doing, Aaron? In Cambodia?' Javier's voice was perfectly polite, and chilling.

'I was filming a documentary on malaria.' *And fantasising about your girlfriend.*

Tina was starting to take on a little of Ella's deer-in-the-headlights look. Sensing the undercurrents, no doubt. 'So, Javier,' Tina said, 'are you able to share with us a little about…about… your experience?'

Javier smiled at her, but to Aaron it looked almost dismissive.

'I was not badly treated,' Javier said. 'Just not free. But not, perhaps, a subject for tonight. Tonight is a celebration, you see. Ella and I…' He stopped, smiled again, drew Ella nearer.

How much closer could he *get* her, anyway? Aaron wondered furiously as he watched Ella.

But she wouldn't meet his eyes. Wouldn't meet anyone's eyes.

'Ella and I would like to share our news,' Javier said, and raised Ella's hand to kiss the palm. 'Ella has done me the honour of accepting my proposal of marriage.'

Aaron caught the sparkle on Ella's finger, and turning away, swallowed the rest of his Scotch in one swig.

Aaron hadn't come looking for Ella.

Didn't want to be alone with her. Not now. When he felt so raw.

And yet there she was, in the kitchen, straightening up after putting something in the fridge.

And there he was. In the kitchen. Forgetting why.

He must have made some sound because she straightened. Turned. The fridge door swung closed behind her.

For a moment Aaron couldn't breathe.

'How are you, Aaron?' she asked quietly.

'Fine.' The word sounded as though it had been bounced into an airless room.

'And Kiri?'

'Fine. He misses you.'

He saw her swallow. She said nothing. Well, what did he expect her to say?

Aaron took a step closer to her. 'There were no consequences? I mean as a…a result of—'

'I know what you mean. I told you I was on the Pill. But just in case, I'm waiting…' Stop. Another swallow. 'I mean, I'm not doing anything… I'm not…with…' She drew an audible breath. 'Until I know.'

'That's good,' Aaron said, miraculously understanding. 'I mean, is it good? Yes, I guess it's good. I guess it's…' Nope. He couldn't finish that.

Silence.

Ella was turning the engagement ring round and round on her finger. 'How's Rebecca? Rehab? How's it going?'

'It's not. She left early; with a drug-addicted film producer. Never anything mundane for Rebecca.'

'Oh, I'm so sorry.'

He rubbed a hand behind his neck. 'Just one thing. I told her about you, about us. In case…'

Ella was fidgeting—which he'd never seen her do. Playing with the damned ring. 'Does that mean…? Does everyone know about us?' she asked.

'No. Nobody else. And Rebecca isn't talking—except to her publicist, who's working out how to go public with the film producer.'

'It's just…Javier's the jealous type. I don't want him to… You know what I mean.'

'I'll fix it so nothing rebounds on you, I promise. And I guess there's nothing to say, anyway. You're engaged.'

Another awful silence.

Aaron took one step closer. 'Have you picked a date? For the wedding?'

'No. Not yet.'

'Why are you doing it, Ella?'

She held out her hands. Imploring. 'How could I say no? How could I refuse him anything after what he's been through?'

He had a few pithy answers for that—but found he couldn't voice them, not when she looked so tormented. 'I'm glad you're not sleeping with him,' he said instead.

He took one more step, close enough now to take her hands, hold them. 'And I know that's unworthy, Ella, but I've discovered I'm not good at giving in gracefully.'

'This is not doing us any good, Aaron.' Ella ried to pull her hands free, but Aaron held on. Let me go. If you don't, I don't know how I'll bear it.'

He pulled her hands against his chest, held hem there. 'Ella, we need to talk.'

'We are talking.'

'Not here, not like this.'

'I can't. I need to get back in there.' She pulled ler hands free. '*Please*, Aaron. It's very difficult just now. Please.'

'*Porque estas tardano tanto?*'

Both Aaron and Ella turned towards the doorway, where a frowning Javier was standing.

'I'm coming now,' she said in English, and walked out of the room, pausing just outside the kitchen door to wait for Javier to join her.

'*Andante, te seguire pronto,*' he said.

Ella looked at Aaron quickly, nervously, then as quickly away. 'All right,' she said.

Javier moved further into the kitchen. He looked Aaron over and seemed to find nothing there to worry about if his slight sneer was anything to go by.

'You know Ella well.' Statement, not question.

'Yes. I do.'

'You watch her.'

The comment surprised Aaron; he'd been conscious of *not* looking at her all night. 'Do I?'

'I can understand. She is beautiful.'

Aaron was silent.

Javier smiled, but it wasn't a friendly smile. 'She is beautiful, and she is mine.'

'If she's yours, what's your problem?'

'I just want it to be clear. So, I think you were bringing the cheese? I'm here to help.'

Cheese. Of course. He had offered to go to the kitchen and get the cheese.

When the two men returned to the dining room, Ella smiled blindingly at her fiancé— the mouth-only version, ha!—put her hand over Javier's when he paused by her chair and touched her shoulder, then moved her chair a smidgeon closer to his when he sat beside her.

Ella's hand kept disappearing under the table and Aaron guessed she was giving Javier's thigh an intermittent pat. Probably reassuring him that she was not remotely attracted to the brooding thug at the other end of the table who now, perversely, couldn't seem to keep his eyes off her.

Which word was stronger—disaster or catastrophe?

Because he was designating this dinner party
a catastrophic disaster or a disastrous catastrophe—whichever was worse.

# CHAPTER FIFTEEN

WHEN ELLA'S CELLPHONE trilled the next morning and Aaron's name flashed, she felt a wash of emotion that was a weird hybrid of joy and anxiety.

'Hello? Ella?'

Ella gasped. *Not* Aaron. 'Kiri! Is everything all right?'

'Where are you, Ella?'

'I'm at Tina's darling, why?'

'We're going to see Mum, and I want to say goodbye. But Dad says you're too busy.'

'Where's Dad?'

'Filming.' Giggle. 'He forgot his phone.'

Her heart swelled with longing. 'When do you leave, Kiri?'

'Soon.'

Which was kid-speak for any time. Tomorrow. Next week. An hour.

Ella bit her lip, thinking. Aaron was on set so the coast was clear. Javier was out, and he didn't have to know. The apartment was within walking distance. Could she do this? See Kiri once more? 'What about if I come over now?' Ella found herself asking.

'Yes!' Kiri said, excited. 'I painted you a picture. Of you and me.'

'Well, I have to see that!' she exclaimed. 'I'll be there soon.'

It didn't take long for Aaron to realise he'd left his phone at home. He felt guilty that he'd be late to the set, because Brand had to head to York in the afternoon to check out locations for an evening shoot, and the schedule was already tight, but he just had to turn back for it. After Kiri's dengue fever episode Aaron liked to be instantly contactable at all times.

Aaron raced into the apartment. 'Jenny?' He called out, and hurried into the living room. 'I forgot my phone, so—' He broke off, and his heart leapt so savagely he couldn't catch his breath.

Ella. Here.

She was sitting with Jenny and Kiri, one of Kiri's paintings in her hands, but she seemed to be holding her breath as her beautiful violet eyes rose to his and stuck there.

Jenny, looking from one to the other of them, murmured something about Kiri needing something. She took Kiri by the hand, led him from the room.

Ella shrugged awkwardly. 'Sorry,' she said, putting down the painting and getting to her feet. 'But he called and I... He said you were leaving?'

'We are—in a few days. Rebecca overdosed. I've got to make sure she's okay.'

'Oh, Aaron.'

'But there's a bright side. It scared her. She's heading back to Trust.'

'That's good. Great.'

'And I'm going to meet Scott too.'

'Scott?'

'The film producer. He's with her. Thank heavens he seems to be on track. She says it's serious between them, and I need to think about what that means for Kiri.'

He could smell her. His heart was aching. He couldn't seem to stop his hand moving up to rub his chest, not that it ever made a difference to the pain.

'We're going to move to LA once the film is

done,' he said. 'To support her. I had an audition there a while back, and I've got a callback, so hopefully...'

'That's great.' Ella smiled—that infuriating smile that didn't reach her eyes. She picked up her bag, preparing to leave. 'I'll be moving, too. Spain.'

'Not LA?'

She shook her head vehemently. 'Not LA. So maybe this time fate will do the right thing and keep us out of each other's way, huh?'

She laughed, but Aaron had never felt less like laughing, and her own dwindled away until she was staring at him, equally silent.

Aaron watched her closely. 'So, we're going to stand here, are we, Ella, and smile and laugh and pretend we don't mean anything to each other? Because I don't think I can do it.'

Her eyes widened. 'Don't,' she said. 'You and Rebecca and Kiri have a long path ahead of you. You need to concentrate on that.'

'And you have to concentrate on martyring yourself, is that it?'

'Stop it, Aaron. Loyalty is not martyrdom. I *owe* Javier this.'

'Two years apart, and then suddenly you get engaged? What do we even know about him?'

'*We* don't need to know anything. Only I do.'

'I told you I'd be waiting for you. And then—'

'Waiting for what? Don't throw Rebecca's new man in my teeth as though that's supposed to make a difference. You've just told me you're following her to America. Where does that leave me? Where?'

He crossed the floor to her. 'I *hoped* in LA. Close to me. Where we could work it out.'

'Oh, spare me. I'd just be carrying two loads of guilt—leaving Javier when he needs me, and being your bit on the side. Well, I'm not doing it.' She paced. One step. Two. Three. Back. 'I knew this would happen. Keep it simple, you said. Casual. And then you proceeded to make it anything but. I tried to make you leave me alone. Sydney, Cambodia, London—every time. Why couldn't you? Why?'

'Because.' *Oh, great answer. Who wouldn't buy that?*

She looked, rightly, incredulous. 'That's an answer?' She turned away, tearing her hands through her hair as though her head was aching.

'All right, I'll tell you why. Because I'm in love with you.'

She spun back to face him. Her mouth formed a silent 'O'. She seemed incapable of speech.

'It's true,' Aaron said, and felt a sense of wonder himself. 'I couldn't leave you alone, because I loved you. I *love* you.'

'I don't want you to.'

'You don't get to dictate to me on this, Ella. If I could have dictated *myself* out of it, I would have. Because, I can assure you, it's not something I wanted either.'

She backed away a step. 'It's just proximity. Because I'm here. And I threw myself at you.'

He laughed harshly. 'Except that I've been lugging it around since Cambodia.' It was true. True! Since *Cambodia*. Why hadn't he realised it before? 'And I'm the one who was doing the throwing,' he continued. 'Always, always me. You were the one running. And I'll tell you this: it's a pain in the butt. *You're* a pain in the butt most of the time, with your bad-girl routine and your secrets. But...' he shook his head '...I love you.'

'Well, stop it. This is a mess. We're a mess. Just as predicted.' Her breath hitched. 'And I—' She broke off, rubbed her hands over her face again. 'This is so frustrating. Why do we do this to each other? Why can't we ever have a normal discussion?'

'I think it's because I love you, Ella.'

'Stop saying that.'

'And I think it's because you don't want to hear it, so you prefer to fight.'

She did that thing where she got herself together, visibly changing from distraught to pale and blank and cool. 'Remember what I said about Disneyland? That it's a blast as long as you remember it isn't real? Let's just say we've had too many turns on the teacups. Your head will stop spinning soon.'

'No, it won't, Ella. My head will still be spinning. My heart will still be aching. And I will still be in love with you.'

She looked at him coldly. 'Then just be happy I'm refusing to help you mess up your life.'

## CHAPTER SIXTEEN

ELLA HAD AN uncomfortable night.

Aaron loved her. *Loved* her.

But it didn't change anything. Because with Brand stuck in York and Tina needing a distraction from her constant back pains, it was *Javier* who took her and her sister out for dinner. It was *Javier* stopping outside Ella's bedroom door when they got home, kissing her, urging her with that sharp, impatient edge to his voice, *'Let me in, Ella. It's time, Ella. Why not, Ella?'*

Why not, Ella? Because Aaron loved her. How was she supposed to sleep with anyone else, knowing that?

It was a relief when Javier left the house after breakfast the next morning, so she didn't have to feel the heavy weight of his dark eyes on her, silently accusing her, questioning her, beseeching her.

Tina was restless, and irritable, and uncomfortable. Demanding a cappuccino from a particular café, which Ella took herself off to buy and bring back so Tina didn't have to get out of her night-gown. Ella hoped Brand's train was on time. She had a nervous feeling Tina's persistent backache meant the baby was preparing to introduce itself to its parents, and Tina would make Brand's life hell if he missed even a second of her labour.

The thought made her laugh as she walked into the house, takeaway coffee in hand. It always amused her to think of Brand—for whom the term alpha male could have been coined—as putty in her sister's hands. Because that's what—

The coffee cup slipped through Ella's fingers. 'Tina!' she cried, and ran towards her sister's crumpled form at the foot of the stairs.

Tina groaned.

Ella closed her eyes, silently thanking every deity she could think of. And then she crouched beside her sister. 'How many times do you have to fall down the stairs before you learn that you do *not* hurry when you're about to give birth?' Ella demanded. 'Brand is going to maim everyone in sight if anything happens to you.'

'It was only the last couple of stairs. I was feeling so awful, and I'm having those horrible Braxton-Hicks things, and I thought I'd go back to bed. So shut up, Ella, and just help me up.'

'Let me check you out first,' Ella said, but Tina was already struggling to her feet—only to slump back down again with a sharp cry.

'I can't get up, Ella. I think I sprained my ankle. And I…' She stopped, and her eyes widened as she looked down at herself, at the floor beneath her. 'Ella!'

She sounded scared. And Ella, seeing the puddle pooling around her sister, understood. Tina's waters had broken.

'But Brand's not here,' Tina wailed, and then she gasped and grabbed Ella's hand. A long, keening moan slipped out between her clenched teeth. 'Oh, no, oh, no,' she whimpered, as her hand loosened after a long moment. 'Ella, I can't do this without Brand. I promised him I wouldn't. He's going to kill me.'

Ella gave a shaky laugh. 'Tina, my darling, the only way he's going to kill you is by kissing you to death. Now, there will be ages to go, but if you're okay to stay there for a moment, I'll go and call the hospital and tell them we're coming in. And I'll call Aaron—he's on standby to drive you to the hospital, right?'

'Okay. Good. No!' Tina grabbed Ella's hand again and held on so tightly Ella wondered if her phalanges were about to snapped in two. Instinctively, she timed the hold. Counting down, counting, counting.

Seventy seconds. The contractions were coming close together. *Uh-oh*.

Tina let go, took a shaky breath.

'Right,' Ella said again, super-calm despite a finger of unease trailing a line down her spine. 'I have to let you go, okay? Just for a moment, to call the hospital.'

Tina, white-faced, nodded. 'And Brand. You have to call Brand. Oh, what's the time? He told me this morning he was trying for an earlier train.'

'I'll try. Just wait, okay?'

Ella raced for the phone and let the private hospital where Ella and Brand had chosen to deliver their baby know they were on their way in. She tried to call Brand but got his voicemail. Assuming he was out of range, she opted not to leave a message; if he got a message about Tina going into labour the moment he switched on his phone, he'd likely hijack the train and make the driver go faster!

She came haring back to Tina, who was in the throes of another contraction—*way* too soon. She allowed both her hands to be grabbed, the knuckles crunched, for the duration, but said, 'Try not to hold your breath, Tina. Just breathe, nice and deep and slow.'

Tina gave her a look that promised her a slow death, but she gave it a gasping try. At the end of the contraction Tina looked up at her. 'Did you get Brand?'

'He must be out of range, Tina. But I'm sure he'll be here soon.'

Tina started to cry, and Ella hugged her. 'Shh,' she said, kissing the top of Tina's head. 'Everything's going to be fine. But we need to get you off these hard tiles and clean you up, and I still need to call Aaron— Oh, hang on, someone's at the door.'

Praying it would be someone useful, Ella raced to the door, tugged it open. Aaron—in the process of knocking again—almost fell inside, and slipped on the spilled coffee. 'Whoa,' he said.

'Thank goodness!' Ella said, and dragged him further into the hall.

'Before you say anything, Ella, I'm not stalking you. I promised Brand I'd look in on Tina, so—' He broke off. 'What's happening?'

'It's Tina, she's in full-on labour!' Ella whispered.

At the same time Tina threw out a wobbly, wailing, 'I know, it *suuuucks*,' from the floor at the base of the stairs.

Ella gave Aaron a warning look. 'It does not suck,' she said, all brisk and professional. 'Because the hospital is expecting us and Aaron is going to get the car and Brand is going to arrive, and everything is going to go according to plan.' She smiled brightly at Tina as she hurried back to her—just in time to take her sister's hands as a scream, followed by a string of graphic curses, tore from Tina's throat.

When the contraction finally stopped, Tina was incoherent, so Ella quickly pulled Aaron aside. 'We're not going to make it to the hospital,' she told him.

'What's wrong?' he asked, sharp and serious.

'Her contractions are too close together, they're too intense, and they're lasting too long. I'm thinking precipitous labour.'

'That sounds bad! *Is* that bad?'

'Well, it's fast, and it's going to be very painful.'

'But if we get her into the car straight away?'

Ella was shaking her head before he'd finished. 'No, the way things are heading, we'll be delivering the baby by the side of the road, and that's *not* happening with this baby. I'm calling an ambulance, but childbirth isn't the highest condition on the triage list. So I'm going to get ready here, just in case. And I'm going to need you to help me.'

Aaron looked completely appalled, but he nodded. 'Just tell me what to do.'

'She's twisted her ankle so—'

A scream from Tina interrupted her. Another contraction.

Ella hurried back to her sister, Aaron beside her. Ella gripped her sister's hand, uttering useless, placating nothings, until the contraction passed. Then she brushed Tina's sweat-damp hair off her face. 'Right, darling, we're not taking any chances with an Aussie driving in London. I'm calling an ambulance instead, and then we're going to make you comfortable while we wait for it to get here, okay?'

Tina nodded, white with stress and pain and terror.

'Aaron's going to stay with you while I'm gone—just for a minute, okay?'

'Okay,' Tina said, sounding pitiful.

Ella drew Aaron aside again. 'Just keep her calm. Encourage her to breathe, deep and slow, deep and slow, but get ready for some screaming.'

'I can take it,' he said.

Tina, eyes glazed, wasted no time in grabbing Aaron's hand as he dropped beside her, squeezing tightly through another fierce contraction. Ella waited, roughly timing through a scream, scream, scream, to the whimper and slump. Ninety seconds.

'Hello, Hercules!' Aaron said admiringly. 'I need to get me some of whatever it is you're eating, bruiser.'

As Ella raced for the phone, she heard Tina give a strangled laugh. She gave another silent prayer of thanks, for Aaron's arrival. Aaron would look after her sister in every way possible—her health, her spirits, her dignity. What more could you ask for at a time like this?

Three calls later, the ambulance, Tina's private obstetrician and another fruitless try for Brand, and she raced up the stairs as another agonising contraction ripped through her sister, with Aaron encouraging her to scream her lungs out if that's what she felt like doing. Not exactly keeping her calm, but Ella had the felling Aaron had the right of it. If Tina wanted to scream her way through, let her!

Ella grabbed an armload of sheets, towels and blankets. She added a fresh nightgown. She then picked up several pairs of sterile surgical gloves from her ever-ready supply, a bandage for Tina's ankle, scissors, rubbing alcohol and an assortment of cotton wool and gauze pads. She winced as she heard Tina's wailing cry as another contraction hit her.

She juggled the goods into a semi-manageable pile in her arms and descended the stairs again. Halfway down, when Tina was silent again, she heard Aaron say, 'You know, Tina, women have been giving birth for thousands of years—and *you're* the one who gets to have Ella personally presiding over the action. How cool is that?'

'Very cool,' Tina gasped out, and met Ella's eyes as she arrived at the bottom of the stairs. 'Very, very cool.' She mouthed, 'I love you,' at Ella, and Ella almost cried.

'Love you too,' she mouthed back. And then she took a deep breath and hurried into the library. She shifted the couch so she had room to stand at the end of it, then quickly put down a thick layer of towels, covered them with a sheet, spread more towels where Tina's hips and thighs would go. She propped cushions, stacking more towels close by, and prepared blankets for when they'd be needed. Over the sounds of her sister screaming, she quickly used the rubbing alcohol to clean the surface of Kiri's activity table, then laid out on it everything else she'd brought from upstairs.

By the time she was back at the stairs, Tina was lying on her side, half on Aaron, abusing him for not massaging her in the right spot.

Aaron, accepting the abuse with equanimity, merely looked up at Ella and asked, 'Ready?'

'Ready,' Ella said.

'Tina,' he said, 'I'm going to lift you now, okay?'

Tina, distressed and almost incoherent, shook her head. 'I'm too messy. Look! I can walk. Or hop. Arm. Just your arm.'

'Tina, when did you start being such a girl?' he asked. 'Get over it and put your arms around my neck.' And then he effortlessly gathered Tina close and lifted her. He carried her into the library, oblivious to the amniotic fluid soaking his T-shirt and jeans.

'Can you balance her while I get her changed?' Ella asked.

'Sure, if you promise not to tell Brand I saw her naked,' Aaron said, and that gave Tina a much-needed laugh—quickly choked off as another contraction hit her.

Somehow, Ella and Aaron managed to get her stripped, freshly nightgowned and settled on the couch.

Ella stroked Tina's sodden hair off her face again. 'Shall I tie your hair back?' she asked,

'Yes, it's really annoying me.'

Ella whipped the elastic from her own hair and bundled Tina's heavy mass of ringlets into a ponytail high on her head. 'And now,' she said, 'I'm going to go and wash my hands, while Aaron waits with you.'

Five minutes later she was back. 'Tina, I need to check how dilated you are, okay?'

Tina cast a look in Aaron's direction.

Ella smiled, understanding. 'While I do that, Aaron is going to go and get me an ice pack for your ankle.' She looked quickly at Aaron. 'And I need some string or twine—I think I saw some in the kitchen drawer. And I need bowls and a plastic bag. Oh, and warm water, but you can get that next trip.'

'On it,' he said, and bolted from the room as Tina went mindless with another contraction, her painful, guttural cries making Ella wish she could take the pain for her.

'Ella. Ambulance. Not…going…to get…here,' Tina gasped as the contraction eased.

'I don't think so, darling,' Ella said 'My niece or nephew seems particularly impatient. Like you, always in a damned hurry.'

'Okay, so let's get onto the important question,' Tina panted out. 'Do you…th-think Brand… is going to be upset…when he finds out I'm in love…with Aaron?'

Ella forced a laugh as she snapped on her sterile gloves, marvelling that her sister could crack a joke at such a time—her precious, amazing sister! 'I think Brand is going to be in love with Aaron himself once all this is over,' Ella said, and searched her head for a distraction. 'So, names. I'm thinking Boadicea, Thorberta and Nathene for a girl. Burford, Lindberg and Ogelsby for a boy. Nice, huh?'

But Tina's strained chuckle was cut off by another moaning scream. 'Ella, Ella, I need to push.'

'Just hang on, hang on, darling. Try to breathe through it.'

'Breathe? Don't be so stupid, Ella. I need to push!'

Tina was sprawled, spread-eagled, with one leg off the couch. Ella positioned herself between her sister's thighs as Tina pushed, pushed hard. She lifted the sheet she'd draped over her sister's legs and, as soon as the contraction eased, inserted her fingers to find—

*Oh, no.* 'Tina, darling, I can feel the baby's head,' she said.

'What? What?' Tina panted.

'The baby's well and truly on the way. I think we can assume all those back pains you had yesterday weren't back pains, they were labour pains, so...'

But Tina was having another contraction, so Ella shut up, caught her sister as she surged up off the couch, held her and let her yell.

'You were saying?' Tina asked weakly, as she sagged back limply. But almost immediately another contraction hit her, and Ella held onto her again and simply breathed, hoping to calm her.

'I'm going to kill Brand. Kill him!' Tina screamed.

Aaron, coming back into the room loaded up with everything Ella had asked for, said, 'Let me do it for you.'

Tina's laugh turned into another screech, and then it was roller-coaster time.

The contractions had Tina in their vicious grip and wouldn't let her go. She was sweating gallons, and Aaron stayed by her side, hanging onto her hand when she needed it, wiping her brow, occasionally leaning over to wipe Ella's too.

Ella had gloved up again, and this time when Tina said she had to push she told Tina to go ahead, because nothing was going to slow this baby down.

All modesty had fled. Tina just wanted the baby out, even if Aaron had to reach in and yank it through the birth canal—which Aaron pronounced himself ready to do, only to be punched and to be told not to be such an idiot.

Ella was staring between her sister's legs. 'The head is crowning,' she said, very calmly. 'Not long now.'

The house phone was ringing. Then Ella's. Then Aaron's. All were ignored.

More contractions. 'Now push, Tina, push now.'

Phones ringing again. One after the other. Once again ignored.

Another contraction. Pushing, pushing, panting, pushing. Tina was shaking. 'Here comes the baby's head,' Ella said. 'Try to stop pushing now, Tina. Stop, the head is here. It's here, Tina.' Ella checked quickly to ensure there was no cord wrapped around the baby's neck. Breathed a sigh of relief. 'Beautiful. Oh, Tina, so beautiful.'

Aaron was holding a weeping Tina's hand, whispering encouragement, kissing her forehead, tears in his eyes, while Ella was supporting the baby's head.

Phones. Ignored.

'One more push and it will all be over,' Ella said, as the baby's head rotated to one side as though it knew what it was doing. And then one shoulder emerged, and the other, and the baby shot into Ella's hands like a bullet. Ella was crying, Tina was crying, Aaron was crying.

'It's a girl,' Ella announced, and, supporting the tiny baby's head and neck carefully, she tilted her to enable any fluids to drain from her nose and mouth.

The baby, eyes wide open like she was completely outraged, gave a strong, angry cry, and Ella quickly checked that she was pink right down to her extremities, her limbs were strong and flexed and that basically she was alert and perfect and gorgeous. Tina held out her arms, and Ella laid the baby on her mother's chest.

Ella checked the wall clock as she took off her gloves. Forty-five minutes from the time she'd spilled that coffee in the hall to the birth of her niece. Incredible! 'Aaron, just pull Tina's nightgown down a little, off her shoulders. Tina, that will let you be skin to skin with the baby. It will help release oxytocin in your body, which will make the placenta slip out faster.'

Judging by the delirious look on Tina's face, Aaron could have done anything just then and she wouldn't have known it. As Aaron adjusted Tina's nightdress, Ella drew a blanket up over the baby's back, making sure Tina, who was shivering, was covered too.

'What can I do next?' Aaron asked, looking at the blood soaking the towels underneath Tina.

'The blood's nothing to worry about, Aaron.'

He passed a shaking hand over his eyes. 'Thank goodness.'

'There is just the placenta to go, if you can pass me that bowl,' she said.

'And then do we get to cut the cord?' Aaron asked.

*We.* Such a little word, but it made Ella want to kiss him. 'When it's stopped pulsing, if the ambulance isn't here.' She ran a tired hand across her forehead. 'But first—the phones, Aaron. I'll bet it was Brand. Can you—?'

But Aaron didn't have to do anything, because Brand erupted into the room, wild-eyed, followed by two paramedics. 'What the hell—?' he started, and then came to a dead stop. His mouth dropped open as he stared at Tina. Then he rushed forward, fell to his knees on the floor beside the couch. 'Tina?' He sounded awed and shaken. 'How did this happen?'

Teary, exhausted, but smiling, Tina reached out a hand, and touched his cheek. Ella and Aaron shared a look as Brand grabbed Tina's hand, pressed a kiss to the palm—just a simple kiss and yet it was so intimate.

One of the paramedics came over to confer with Ella, who quickly provided details of the morning's drama.

And then Ella realised she and Aaron were *de trop*.

The baby was being checked; the placenta would be delivered and bagged; Tina would be taken care of. Brand was cooing at his wife and daughter.

With a smile at Aaron Ella inclined her head towards the door, and the two of them left the library. The stood in the hall, looking at each other. And then Aaron said, 'I never did get the warm water.'

Ella started to laugh.

'And where the hell did I put the ice pack?' he asked.

And then they were both laughing. They laughed, laughed, laughed, as Aaron—covered in dried amniotic fluid—pulled Ella—covered in blood—into his arms. He buried his face in her loose hair. They clung together for a long moment, before drawing apart slowly.

Euphoric, shaken, exhausted, they stared at each other. Ella's heart was aching, her breath jammed in her throat with a lurching, desperate need to touch him. To huddle against him and weep and sigh and just *have*.

Brand broke the spell, exploding out of the

ibrary with the same energy with which he'd entered it. 'I cut the cord,' he announced proudly.

Next moment, he was grabbing Ella, hugging her. Ella could feel him shaking. 'I love you,' he whispered in her ear.

'I love you too, Brand,' Ella whispered back, and kissed his cheek. 'And your beautiful wife, and your adorable baby girl.'

'Audrey Ella McIntyre—that's her name,' he said. And then he freed one arm and reached for Aaron, dragged him in. 'Mate,' he said. Just one word, but it said everything, because in it was joy and love and excitement and gratitude.

'Do we get to smoke a cigar now?' Aaron joked, and was dragged closer still.

'You're an uncle now—no smoking,' Brand said, in a suspiciously husky voice.

Then Tina and the baby were being wheeled out of the library, and Brand, laughing maniacally, was off like an arrow as he followed his wife and daughter out of the house.

Aaron cocked an eyebrow at Ella. 'So, can I clean up that spilled coffee over there and make you a new one?' he asked.

He was very conscious of the butterflies swooping in his gut, now he was alone with her.

Butterflies? Did a grown man even *get* butterflies?

He *never* got butterflies.

Ella looked at him, biting her bottom lip. Was she going to say no?

'It wasn't my coffee. It was Tina's.'

'So I *can't* make you one?'

'Yes, yes, of course you can,' she said, but she looked nervous. 'I'll clean the spill later, though.' She took a deep breath. 'Right now, I really, really do need coffee. Just as soon as I wash myself up.'

Aaron did what he could to clean himself up, then made his way to the kitchen. He wondered what kind of conversation they could have after delivering a baby together. And after yesterday's conversation, when he'd told her he loved her.

*So, Ella, how's it going? Decided you love me yet?*

His smile twisted. Maybe not.

Aaron realised he was standing there in a trance, looking at her while he rubbed his hand over his heart. He hated it that he did that when he looked at her, whenever he even *thought* of her. His T-shirts were all going to start showing wear and tear in that one spot.

He busied himself with boiling water, setting out cups, spooning instant coffee. Ella came in and took a seat at the kitchen counter.

Aaron handed her a mug. 'So, Ella, do you need…do you need…anything? From me? Now? Do you need…' *Me? Me, me, me? Do you need me, Ella?* 'Um…anything?'

'No. It's just…'

Just her voice. Her husky Yankee voice was enough to make him melt. 'Just?'

'I can't believe I was jealous—of my own sister, of this baby. Because now…' She stopped, shook her head. 'It's just so perfect. Isn't it? Perfect!'

'Yes it's perfect, so take off the hair shirt for a while, Ella, hmm?' He reached over, touched her hair, just once. 'Funny, isn't it? Brand had every specialist in Europe on speed dial, and all it took was you.'

'I was so scared,' she said, and he heard the steadying breath she dragged in. 'I don't know what I would have done if you weren't here.'

'Nobody would have known you were scared. You're just amazing, Ella. But, hey, if you want to fall apart now it's all over, here I am,' he said. 'You can cry all over me.'

Ella looked at him and smiled—that glorious smile, with her mouth and her eyes and her heart and her soul.

*That* smile.

It told him that, regardless of what they wanted or didn't want, they were connected.

It was fate.

'Oh, Aaron,' she said.

He thought she would say more, but then, outside the room, there was a quick burst of Spanish.

'I'd better go,' Ella said, and leaving her coffee, untouched, on the counter, she rushed from the kitchen.

Hmm. Fate had a lousy sense of timing, all things considered.

When Aaron and Kiri walked into Tina's hospital room that night, Ella was there, holding the sleeping baby.

Her eyes lit up when she saw him and his heart felt like it was doing a triple back somersault with a full twist. He caught himself doing that hand-rubbing thing over it again and had a bad eeling it wasn't a habit he was going to kick any ime soon.

'Hello, Kiri,' she said. 'Aaron.' She looked kind )f shy. It was entrancing. 'Recovered from to-lay's high drama, then?'

'Yes,' he said. Not exactly a scintillating con-versationalist tonight, but after the intimacy .hey'd shared at Audrey's birth—even though hey'd been so focused on Tina they'd barely spo-ken to each other through the experience—he found himself tongue-tied. He was just so in love with her. He wondered how he hadn't seen his obsession with her for what it was sooner.

Love. If he'd admitted it to himself in Cam-bodia, they'd be married and she'd be pregnant by now; although, after today, how he'd actually *'ive* through Ella in labour he didn't know, and nobody would have the power to keep her from him—not even her.

'Ah, Kiri, my favourite boy,' Tina said. 'Did you come to see me or Audrey?'

'You *and* Audrey,' Kiri said, approaching the bed. His eyes were huge, staring at the baby.

'Smooth talker,' Tina said, laughing. 'Ella, let Kiri see her properly.'

Ella settled herself in the chair next to Tina's bed and beckoned Kiri closer.

When Kiri was beside her he asked, 'Can I touch her?'

'Yes,' Ella said. 'In fact...' She shot Tina a questioning look and waited for Tina to nod. 'You can hold her. But you'll have to sit very still in this chair. Can you do that?'

'Give Tina the picture first, mate,' Aaron told him, and Kiri handed it to his father without taking his eyes off the baby.

Aaron laughed as he presented it to Tina. 'I think we know where his priorities lie, Tina, and they're not with you or me—or even Ella, who used to be his favourite up until two minutes ago.'

Ella settled Audrey on Kiri's lap and positioned his arm so that it was firmly under her head. 'She doesn't have a strong neck yet, so you need to be careful that you hold her head like this. All right?'

Kiri nodded. Audrey didn't fret, just accepted this little boy who was holding her as though it was the biggest adventure of his life. Then Kiri leaned his face down to the baby and softly kissed her forehead.

Ella looked at Aaron. Aaron looked at Ella. Aaron reckoned an outsider could have mistaken them for the parents of both children.

Tina cleared her throat. 'Ella,' Tina said, 'why don't you take those flowers from Aaron?'

'Sure,' Ella said, and there was relief in her voice. 'I'll go and cajole another vase out of the nursing staff.'

Aaron perched on the edge of Tina's bed, watching Kiri with the baby.

'I'm so grateful, Aaron, for what you did today,' Tina said.

'I didn't do anything.'

'You kept me calm, you rubbed my aching back, you let me squeeze your fingers, you took more verbal abuse than any man should have to.' Slight pause. 'And you gave my sister strength, just by being there.'

Aaron shook his head. 'Ella didn't need me, Tina.'

Tina looked at him, like he was a puzzle. 'Men really are stupid, aren't they?' she asked. 'Look, Aaron, now that you've seen my lady bits being stretched to oblivion, I feel I know you well enough to be blunt with you. So I'm just going to come right out and ask you: what are you going to do about Ella?'

Aaron jerked so suddenly his leg slipped off the bed. 'I—I— She—'

'Yes, you're as articulate on the subject as she is. Look—you're divorced. Can you make like you really, really mean that, Aaron? And then get my sister away from that man.'

'I thought you liked him?'

'And that's what's stopping you, is it? The way you think I feel?'

'Ella doesn't feel that way about me.'

She fixed him with an incredulous stare. 'Don't be an imbecile. She won't *admit* to feeling that way about you while you've got a wounded animal to look after. Apologies to Rebecca, but you get the picture.'

'She won't leave Javier.'

Tina gave an exaggerated sigh. 'Stupid and so damned *aggravating*. All right, then, forget Ella. Stay in your rut, juggling all your balls and making sure none of them accidentally hits another while they're in the air, and let Javier have her. Because she will marry him, you know. She has a greater capacity for pity than Mother Teresa ever did. Oh, well, at least they'll have good-

ooking kids.' She turned to Kiri. 'Kiri, sweetheart, I think Daddy wants a turn. You come and
ell me about this lovely painting.'

Aaron took that to mean she couldn't bear to
speak to him.

He lifted Audrey out of Kiri's arms and stood
there, staring down at the newborn and rocking
her in his arms. And wondering…

Ella smiled at him as she came back into the
room. 'Got a vase,' she announced, and positioned it, flowers already arranged, on the window ledge.

'I think Audrey's smiling at me,' Aaron said.

'If she is, Brand will beat you to a pulp,' Tina
said, sounding like she was relishing the thought.

*Ouch.* 'All right, maybe she's not smiling,' he
said. Her tiny mouth opened and closed a few
times. 'Is that what you'd call gurgling, maybe?'

Ella laughed. 'No,' she said.

'Hmm. Man, she smells good,' he said after a
moment.

'Yes. Babies always smell delicious.' She made
a last adjustment to the flowers and then held out
her arms for Audrey. 'Time for her to go back to
bed,' she said. Aaron gently laid the baby in her
arms so she could place her in her bassinette.

*Oh, Lord*, he thought as that mesmerising scen of Ella's hit his nostrils. She smelled more deli cious than a thousand babies.

'Where's Javier tonight?' Tina asked, all in nocence.

'He's out with some of his friends. There' a new medical mission in Ethiopia and...' Sh shrugged.

Tina raised her eyebrows. The picture of disap proval. 'So he's going back to Africa. Would tha be before or after you're married, Ella?'

'I don't know, Tina. I guess he'll tell me wher he tells me.'

A snort from the bed. 'Very wifely of you, wait ing to be told. But not very Ella.'

'It's not like that.'

Another snort.

Aaron judged it time to step into the breach 'I have something to talk to Ella about.' he saic to Tina. 'Can we leave Kiri with you for a few minutes?'

Tina gave him a beaming smile. 'Go. Please. Go.'

'I guess we'll go, then,' Ella said dryly.

Ella and Aaron paused outside the room. And

hen Ella burst out laughing. 'Is it hormones, or
did I miss something?'

'You missed something. I don't know how to
break this to you, but I don't think she's crazy
about your fiancé.'

'Oh, I know that. Subtle, she isn't.'

'What happened?'

'Just a vibe, I think.' She looked hesitant.
Do you think we can grab that coffee, without
launching World War Three across the table?'

'I'm game if you are. I'll try to keep it at
skirmish level rather than a heavy mortar attack.'

'Then I'll keep my grenade pins just half-
pulled. Cafeteria, then? The coffee will be awful,
but—'

'Cafeteria,' he agreed.

Ella wondered what the hell she was doing.

In a cafeteria, with Aaron, on purpose. Aaron,
whose last attempt at drinking a cup of coffee
with her had ended with her running to Javier.
Aaron, whom she'd basically ordered not to love
her.

'So what's the vibe?' Aaron asked, sliding a
cup of coffee across the table to her.

Her mind went momentarily blank.

'Javier, Tina?' Aaron prompted. 'The vibe?'

'Oh. Well.' She stalled, taking a sip of coffee 'She says he's too controlling.'

'Is she right?'

'He…' Another sip of coffee.

'What's wrong, Ella?'

'Huh?'

'If you can take two sips of that coffee and not make an icky face, then you're not tasting it. Which means you're distracted. So, what's wrong?'

What was *wrong* was having this conversation with Aaron. But somehow, bizarrely, it was *right* too.

'Javier is…different,' she started, hesitantly. 'From what I remember, I mean.'

Aaron leaned back in his chair. 'And we're not talking good different.'

It wasn't a question, but Ella answered anyway. 'I think, no. But I don't really know yet. He won't talk about what happened. It makes it…hard.'

She watched as he absorbed that. His fists had clenched. And there was something in his eyes that urged caution.

'Go on,' he said.

She shook her head. 'This is a bad idea, talking to you about this. After...well, after—'

'After I declared my undying love and you threw it back in my face?'

'Yes, definitely a mistake.' She started to get to her feet.

He reached across the table, gripped her wrist. 'Sorry, Ella. If I promise to not let my skyrocketing testosterone get in the way, will you tell me?'

She relaxed into her seat. Nodded. Then she licked her lips, nervous. 'I told you he's the jealous type. Well, he *really* is.'

'You mean, of me?'

'Oh, yes. Even the thought of you helping me today with the baby? Well, let's just say it didn't go down well.'

'But that's insane.'

'And it's not just that. Not just you. He's jealous of everyone. Every man I talk to. Every man who looks at me.'

'Frankly, he's an insecure dirtbag.'

That surprised a laugh out of her. 'That's your testosterone not getting in the way, is it?'

'But he really *is* a dirtbag. Jealous of me? I get it. Because I want you. You know it. I know it. Tina and Brand know it. Tinkerbelle the neighbour's Chihuahua knows it. But, Ella, he does realise you're Hollywood-gorgeous, doesn't he? Every heterosexual man on the planet would take a second look at you. Come on! He's going to be living in hell if he can't cope with that—or he's going to make *you* live in hell because you won't be able to stop it. If he knew you, he'd trust you. So you're basically telling me he doesn't know you.'

Coffee. Sip. Ghastly. Okay, tasting the coffee was a good sign. 'You're so sure you know me that well?'

'I know that much about you. In fact, I'm wishing you were a little *less* faithful the way things are panning out. So, we're back to him being a dirtbag.'

'I haven't exactly been the poster girl for virtue, though, have I?'

'People do all kinds of things to get through tough times. They drink. They play pool with strange men.' Smile. 'They have sex with hunky Australian television stars.' Bigger smile. 'So what? Last time I looked, it wasn't the twelfth century. Nobody expects a twenty-seven-year-old woman to be a virgin, or to enter a convent to wait until her man rises from the dead.' He took her hand. 'Here's the sales pitch for me, just in case you ever end up interested: I wouldn't care if you'd had sex with a thousand men before me, Ella.'

She wanted to both smile and cry, but did neither. 'It wasn't like that, ever. In fact—'

He cut her off with a sharp, 'Hey, stop.'

'Stop?'

'Yes, stop. Don't tell me. And it's not because I'm squeamish either. Or *jealou*s. It's just none of my business. As long as it was *before*. Now, after? Well, that's another story.'

'But it wasn't before, was it?' she said. 'It was after. I had the option of waiting for him and I didn't. I was with you.'

'You are *not* serious, Ella! He was missing for two years; maybe dead. And in my book you *were* waiting. You certainly weren't living.' He squeezed her hand. 'You're not really going all hair shirt on me, are you?'

'I don't think you're the right person to be lecturing me on excessive conscience, Mr Married-Not-Married.' Her shoulders slumped. 'I wish he was more like...' She cleared her throat. 'Nothing.'

'It's "not married". *Not* married. Just to be clear,

in case that's what's stopping you from leaving him and throwing yourself at me.' Pause. 'And it's not nothing, I think.'

She smiled. 'It's just…well, you're very different from Javier. And I think he *would* care that I'd been with you. And I think…' Pause, swallow. 'I think I have to tell him. Don't you?'

He let go of her hand, sat back abruptly. 'How did we end up here? One minute we're talking about your sister's excellent intuition when it comes to fiancés and the next you're getting ready to throw yourself on your sword and confess something that's *none of his business*. Shall I say that again? *None of his business.*'

'But what if he finds out? *After* we're married?'

'Who's going to tell him?' Then Aaron seemed to catch himself. He shook his head, bemused. 'I can't believe I'm saying this! If it sounds like I'm talking you into marrying him, don't listen to me.'

'It just seems dishonest. Knowing how he feels about other men even looking at me, telling him is the honourable thing to do.' She looked Aaron straight in the eye. 'It's what you would do, isn't it?'

'I'd break up with him. That's what I'd do.'

'Be serious.'

'I am. Serious as a sudden home birth.'

'You told Rebecca about us.'

'Rebecca and I are divorced, remember?'

'And when you found out about Rebecca being unfaithful, you forgave her.'

He sighed. 'It's not the same, Ella. It's not as simple as admitting you've been unfaithful—although in your case I'll dispute that to my dying day—and getting a blessing in return for being honest.'

'*You'd* forgive me.'

'As far as I'm concerned, there's nothing to forgive. But that's me. If he's the jealous type, and controlling...' He paused, seemed to be weighing his words. 'Who knows how he'll react?'

She looked at her watch. 'Anyway, we'd better get back to Tina. It's late and you need to get Kiri home.'

They left the cafeteria and walked in silence back to Tina's room.

'Thank you for listening,' she said, stopping him just outside. 'You know, don't you, that I've never been able to talk to anyone the way I talk to you? I *don't* talk to anyone like this. Only you. Do you know how much it means to me to have this?'

She reached up, cupped his cheek, and he pressed his hand over hers.

'You don't need to do this, Ella,' he said.

She removed her hand. 'I do,' she insisted. 'And I have to believe he'll forgive me.'

He blew out a breath. 'He will, if he's not a complete idiot. And, for the record, I'd forgive you anything shy of genocide.' He pursed his lips. 'Nah—I'd forgive you that as well.' He frowned down at her. 'And if he *is* a complete idiot, you've got my number. I told you I loved you and I meant it. And I told you I'd wait for you. I will, Ella.'

His hand was over his heart, rubbing. Ella, noticing it, frowned. 'Are you all right?'

'What?' He looked down, stopped the movement straight away. She was surprised to see a slight flush stain his cheekbones. 'Oh, yes,' he said.

Long pause. 'It's hopeless for us, you know that, Aaron.'

'No, I don't,' he answered. 'And I hope you realise I'm in deep trouble with your sister. She thinks I'm out here convincing you to run away with me.'

'You don't want that, Aaron. Not really. Rebecca needs you. Kiri needs Rebecca. And Javier needs me. That's our lives.'

'You left out who you need, Ella. And who I need. I don't accept that our lives are about what everyone *except* us needs. If you could be a little less martyr-like about it—'

'I am not a martyr.'

'Maybe not all the time, but you're in training. Inconveniently, right after meeting me.' He took her hands in his, forestalling any more protestations. 'Anyway, just don't get married too soon. Make sure you get to know the man a little better first.'

'Ella?'

They broke apart and Ella whirled in the direction of Javier's voice.

Ella hurried towards Javier. 'I'm glad you made it.'

He made no move to touch her. 'Are you?' he asked, keeping his flashing black eyes trained on Aaron, who nodded at him and stayed exactly where he was.

Like he was on sentry duty.

Ella was torn between wanting to thump Aaron and wanting to kiss him. Here he was, protecting her from her fiancé in case Javier didn't like what he'd seen—when, really, what was there to like about it? Seeing your future wife holding another man's hands and gazing at him.

There was going to be an argument. And it wasn't going to be pleasant. But not here.

'Yes, I am,' Ella said, determinedly cheerful. 'Visiting hours are over but they're not too strict. Let's go and see Audrey. She looks just like Tina.' She looked at Aaron. 'Doesn't she?'

'Yes,' Aaron agreed. 'It was good to see you, Ella. I'll just pop in for a moment to say good-bye and collect Kiri, then leave you to it.' With what Ella could only describe as a warning look at Javier, Aaron walked into Tina's room, saying, 'Kiri, time to make tracks.'

Ella started to follow Aaron in but Javier stopped her with a hard grip on her arm. 'First, I think you had better tell me what is going on with you and him,' he said.

'Not in a hospital corridor.' Ella eased her arm free. 'Now, come in and see my sister. See the baby. Then we'll go home. And we'll talk.'

Javier didn't touch her on the way home. Didn't speak to her. Didn't look at her.

Ella dreaded the impending argument. But she longed for it too. Because they had to deal with everything—their pasts, their fears, their insecurities, their hopes—before they took another step towards marriage.

Having Aaron to talk to had made her realise she should never have kept her grief locked in for so long. Being able to talk to someone, confide in someone would have eased two long years of heartache.

So now she was going to talk to *this* man. She was preparing to share her life with him, and she couldn't do that without sharing how the past two years had changed her. And if Javier wouldn't confide in her in return, tell her how he'd stayed sane during two years of captivity…well, she didn't know what she'd do. Because she needed that knowledge. The insight. The trust.

They entered the house, went to Javier's room.

'So talk,' he said, and closed the door.

'I—I guess I should start with—'

'Start with what is going on with Aaron James. Why was he holding your hands?'

Ella stayed calm. 'He was comforting me. That's all.'

'Comforting you *why*?'

Still calm. But she licked her lips. 'Because I had just made a difficult decision.'

'What decision? And why were you with him when you made it? Why not me?'

Okay, not so calm. 'I was with him because the decision concerns you.'

His eyes narrowed. He said nothing. Just waited.

'To explain, I need to go back. To when you were kidnapped, and I tried so hard to find out what happened to you, and nobody could— or would—tell me anything. I wasn't a wife, I wasn't a sister. Nobody knew I was even a girl-friend. I'm not sure anyone would have helped me anyway. Because nobody knew anything. All I could do was wait. And wait. And...wait.'

He hadn't moved a muscle.

'It does something to you, the waiting,' she said, drowning. 'And I know you must know what I mean, because you were waiting too.'

'This is about you, Ella, not me.'

'But you never talk about it. You never—'

'You. Not me,' he rapped out.

She jumped. 'Right. Yes. Well...I—I—'

'Waited for me,' he finished for her, and it was more of a taunt than a statement.

'Yes, I did.'

'And you kept waiting, and waiting, and waiting.'

'Y-yes.'

'Until Aaron James came along.'

She sucked in a breath. Sudden. 'No. At least, yes but…no.'

He looked at her. Utterly, utterly cold. 'Yes but no?'

The snap in his voice had her stomach rioting.

'You slept with Aaron James. Just say it.'

She jumped, jolted. 'I thought you were dead.'

He had started pacing the room. 'You wished I was.'

'No!' she cried. 'Never, ever, ever.' She felt like she was running at a brick wall. It wouldn't yield; only she could. Or try, at least. 'It's over between me and Aaron. He is no threat to you.'

Javier stopped, looked at her, incredulous. 'No threat to me? No *threat*?'

'I will be living in Barcelona, with you. He will be on the other side of the world.'

He shoved her against the wall. 'He is your sister's friend. He will be there, always.' He punched his fist into the wall beside her head. 'You have been denying me what you gave *him*. You introduced him to me. You made a fool of me.'

Ella stayed ultra-still, scared to move. 'I wanted to tell you. I am telling you. Now.'

'Now!' He looked into her face. He was only just holding his fury in check. 'Two years I survived, to come back and learn that you have slept around.'

'Don't say that,' Ella said.

'How do I know that you weren't sleeping with who knows how many men from the moment I was gone? We'd only known each other a few weeks when you slept with me. A woman like you would sleep with anyone. That's what I think you have spent the last two years doing. Now, just admit it, Ella.'

Ella thought of all the things she had planned to tell him tonight. The confession about Aaron, yes, but also about Sann, about her life in despairing limbo. And this is what it had come down to. 'No,' she said quietly. 'I will not admit to that.'

He raised his hand as if to hit her.

Her eyes blazed. 'If you touch me, I will make you sorry you're not still in Somalia,' she said.

'No, I won't hit you,' he said. 'You're not worth it, Ella.'

It took all of Ella's courage to turn from Javier. To walk slowly out of the room, not run, as his curses continued to rain on her.

She sat in her bedroom, shaking. She could hear drawers and cupboard doors slamming. Curses. Wheels on the floor—his bag. There was a pause outside her door. She imagined him coming in…

She held her breath, realised she was trembling like a leaf.

Then another inarticulate curse. Footsteps going down the stairs.

Out of her life.

Even three floors up she heard the front door slam.

'Some things just change,' she whispered to herself, and remembered Aaron saying exactly that to her.

She'd thought it would be comforting to accept that.

Instead, it made her cry.

# CHAPTER SEVENTEEN

*Ella? Ella pick up. It's me.*

*Hellooo? Ella? Why didn't you return my call?*

*Ella, pick up! Come on, pick up!*

Yeah, three messages were probably enough, Aaron decided, catching himself before he could leave a fourth.

He contemplated calling Brand to do some back-door sleuthing—but pictured his lifeless body sporting a variety of blunt and sharp force injuries should Ella get wind of that, and opted to spend the night tossing and turning instead as he wondered how the confession had gone. Whether Javier and Ella were in bed, burying the infidelity hatchet in a lusty bout of lovemaking.

*No!*

He would *not* imagine that.

He would, instead, plan what he would say, how he would act, tomorrow, when he made a last-ditch effort to woo Ella, regardless of what had happened between her sheets tonight.

And screw the best-buddy routine the two of them had enacted at the hospital; he should have whisked her off into the night instead of letting her saunter off with the darkly brooding doctor.

Anyway, enough dwelling on what he should have done. More important was the future.

So, back to what he was going to say to Ella.

And it was suddenly so clear! Why did it have to be three o'clock in the morning when he realised that keeping things simple was not about compartmentalising things to death? Ella in one corner, Rebecca in another, Kiri in a third. Him in the fourth, sashaying back and forth between them. Tina had put it best—he was juggling balls to make sure they didn't ever connect.

Dumb, dumb, dumb.

Because who wanted to juggle for eternity? It was exhausting. You had to stop some time and hold all the balls together in your hands, if you didn't want your arms to fall off.

Yep, it was crystal clear at three o'clock.

He was getting quite poetic.

And perhaps a little maudlin. Because he couldn't help revisiting every stupid argument he and Ella had ever had, wishing he could go back and fix every single one of them to get the right ending.

How arrogant he'd been, to insist they couldn't have a relationship because of his complicated life. Who *didn't* have a complicated life? Ella's was worthy of its own mini-series! All he'd managed to do was give Ella every argument she'd ever need to keep him at arm's length for the rest of their natural lives.

And she knew how to use them.

One. What was good for Rebecca. Well, if Rebecca knew she was the main obstacle to his relationship with Ella, she'd laugh herself sick.

Two. What was good for Kiri. As if being around Ella could ever be bad for him!

Three. His own initial disapproval of her. Short-lived it may have been, but Ella had turned out to be an expert at hurling that at his head.

He wanted to slap himself in the head when he thought back to how he'd made Ella feel like she wasn't good enough to be near his son. Except that he couldn't hit himself hard enough; he'd need some kind of mediaeval mace with all the spiky protuberances to do his self-disgust justice.

Just how was he going to fix the situation?

He could do better. He *would* do better. He

would be sane, articulate, charming, passionate, clever. He would convince her that she belonged with him.

Tomorrow he would prove that love was really simple. Just being in it and grabbing it when it hits you and making your life fit around it, not it fit around your life. *Very* simple.

What time was a decent time to arrive at Brand's, given Tina and Audrey were coming home from the hospital? Just after lunch? That seemed good timing. For a sane, reasonable man who was insanely, unreasonably in love with a woman who held all the cards.

He found that he was rubbing his chest over his heart again.

Man, he hated that.

One look in the mirror the next day had Ella raiding Tina's store of make-up.

She couldn't look like one of the undead for Tina's return from the hospital.

And she would have to handle the news of her break-up with Javier carefully, with no mention of last night's awful showdown, if she didn't want Tina packing the electrical wires and blowtorch in a backpack and going off to hunt Javier down.

But she would, at last, tell her sister everything about the past two years, including what had happened with Sann. She would let her into her pain and grief the way she should have done all along.

And then she would go back to Los Angeles. And she would tell her parents.

And then it would be time for her to move on, and make new memories.

No guilt, no shame.

'She's not here, Aaron.'

Aaron heard the words come out of Brand's mouth but couldn't quite compute.

'Not here?' His eyes widened. 'Then where is she? *How* is she?'

'If it's the break-up with Javier you're talking about, she's fine. I'd go so far as to say she's relieved.'

Aaron felt a wave of intense happiness, until the look on Brand's face registered. 'So when will she be back?' he asked.

And then Brand put his arm around Aaron's shoulder, steered him into the library.

Not promising.

Brand poured Scotch into a glass, held it out

or Aaron. 'Her flight home took off about half an hour ago,' he said.

Aaron took the glass, almost mechanically sipped.

Brand walked over to his desk, plucked a small envelope off it, handed it to Aaron.

*Aaron.*
*I think we've all had enough upheavals for a while so let's not add any more drama. Good luck with Rebecca. And hug Kiri for me.*
*Ella*

He looked up and caught Brand's eye.

'That's it?' he demanded.

'That's it.'

He reread the note.

'Yeah, screw that,' he said. 'When do we wrap up filming?'

'Four weeks.'

'Then that's how long she's got before I go after her.'

'Princess Tina will be pleased,' Brand said, and slapped him on the shoulder.

# CHAPTER EIGHTEEN

ELLA WASN'T HOME.

Aaron almost laughed as he recalled the way he'd played this scene out in his head. He would knock on the door of her apartment. She would open the door, stare at him, smile that dazzling smile—the one that had her heart and soul in it—and then she would leap into his arms and kiss him. She would tell him she loved him, that she couldn't live without him. That she'd been waiting for him.

Very satisfactory.

Except that she wasn't home.

The only romance he'd had so far had involved charming Ella's young gay doorman into letting him into the building.

Well, he'd told Ella more than once he would wait for her. And here he was, waiting.

It had been four weeks. Enough time for Ella to miss him desperately. Enough time for him to get all the elements in place to counteract Ella's martyrish inclinations: Rebecca was doing brilliantly at Trust; her new love affair was steaming ahead and Aaron liked the guy; custody arrangements had been sorted; and Aaron had even managed to nab that lead role in the LA-based detective series he'd auditioned for.

Fate was lining up for him at last.

Now he just had to pray that Ella wasn't about to head off to the Congo or float herself down the Amazon, and life would be perfect.

If he could just get her to say three little words.

He didn't really know if she could say those words. Or feel them.

He heard the elevator, and scrambled to his feet. He'd done this four times already—all false alarms—but, hey, he wasn't about to be found by the love of his life sitting on the floor.

Then he saw her. She was wearing the dress he'd bought her in London. That *had* to be a sign.

He felt those blasted butterflies again. Actually, forget butterflies; these were more like bats. Humongous bats.

He knew the moment she saw him. The hitch in her stride. Then the slow, gliding tread towards him.

'Well,' Ella said inadequately, with the smile that didn't reach her eyes.

All Aaron's optimism dropped through his gut to the floor. 'Don't,' he said. 'Don't smile like that. Not like that. Not now.'

'I don't—'

'And don't say you don't know what I mean. Because you do. Aren't you happy to see me, Ella?'

He heard her suck in a breath. And then she said, 'Is everything…? Is everything okay? Rebecca…'

'In rehab. Taking control. Doing great. But even if her life were off the rails, I'd still be here, Ella. What I would have told you, if you hadn't left London when you did, was that I was going to make things work for us come hell or high water. No matter what was happening with anyone else. Rebecca, Kiri, your family, even Javier—I'd still want you with me. All right, to be honest, I still want to damage one of Javier's cheekbones, so having him in our lives might take a little work.'

'Javier just couldn't forgive. Couldn't even accept. And I realised either he'd changed or I never really knew him. But if you'd seen him, so heroic and caring and brilliant in Somalia, you—'

'Yeah, yeah, don't expect me to get all misty-eyed over his good doctor deeds, Ella. And he had nothing to forgive. I don't want to talk about him. I don't care about him. I only care about you.'

He stepped closer to her. 'I don't know what I'll do if I can't have you. You and I, we're supposed to be together. Can't you feel it? We've learned, both of us, that life isn't about hanging on the sidelines, waiting for things to get better. Or worse. Waiting for fate to come and toss a grenade or a bouquet or a wet fish. I'll catch every grenade, Ella, and I'll still love you. I'll navigate any difficulty to have you.'

She blinked hard. Again. 'Oh.'

'I'll follow you to Sierra Leone or Chad or Somalia or Laos.'

She shook her head. 'It's good old America for a long time to come, so you'll have to think of something else.'

'Hmm. So, what about...?' He held up his hands. They were shaking. 'What about this? Nobody else has ever made me shake just because they were near me, Ella.'

'Are you sure? Are you really sure, Aaron?'

He waved his hands at her. 'Look at them! Like a leaf in a gale.'

'I don't mean— I mean I don't want you to regret me. I don't want to become one more responsibility to bear. And you know, better than most, I've hardly been a saint, so I'd understand—'

'Stop talking like that!' He started undoing his shirt.

'What about Kiri? How will Rebecca take it?'

'Kiri loves you, and as for Rebecca—was I just talking about not caring? But if it will get you over the line, I swear I'll get her blessing in writing. My sisters—they've posted an embarrassing video on YouTube begging you to take me—wait until you see it. And I've already gone and—'

'What are you doing?' she asked, seeming to notice at last that he was removing his shirt. 'I'm not— I don't— I— Oh!'

'Do you like it?'

Ella came forward, put her hands on his chest. He'd had her name tattooed across his chest. Her name. Bold and beautiful.

And something else.

Dropping from the A over his left pectoral muscle was a gold ring that looked like it was enterng his skin where his heart was, anchoring her name there. Her fingers traced it. 'Oh, Aaron. Yes, I like it.'

'I'll ink my whole body for you Ella, if you want.'

'No, just this,' she said. 'It looks…permanent.' She put her head on one side, querying him. 'Is it?'

'The things I'll do to get a green card,' Aaron quipped, and then gathered her in, held her against his chest, tilted her face up to his. 'Yes, it's permanent. And so are you. Are you ready, Ella, my darling? You know I want you. You know I'm obsessed, besotted, madly and wildly in love with you. Tell me you feel the same. Tell me you're ready. Come on, Ella. Say it. Say it.'

'I love you. And, yes,' she breathed. And then she smiled and her face lit up like the sun. Bright and gold and glowing. His smile. Just for him. I'm ready.'

He closed his eyes. Breathed in. Out. Opened his eyes. 'Then let's get inside. I want to have my way with you— No, wait! I want you to have your way with me. Hang on, I want— Oh, Ella, just open the door.'

\* \* \* \* \*

# MILLS & BOON®
## Large Print Medical

## May

| | |
|---|---|
| PLAYING THE PLAYBOY'S SWEETHEART | Carol Marine |
| UNWRAPPING HER ITALIAN DOC | Carol Marine |
| A DOCTOR BY DAY... | Emily Forbe |
| TAMED BY THE RENEGADE | Emily Forbe |
| A LITTLE CHRISTMAS MAGIC | Alison Robert |
| CHRISTMAS WITH THE MAVERICK MILLIONAIRE | Scarlet Wilso |

## June

| | |
|---|---|
| MIDWIFE'S CHRISTMAS PROPOSAL | Fiona McArthu |
| MIDWIFE'S MISTLETOE BABY | Fiona McArthu |
| A BABY ON HER CHRISTMAS LIST | Louisa George |
| A FAMILY THIS CHRISTMAS | Sue MacKa |
| FALLING FOR DR DECEMBER | Susanne Hampton |
| SNOWBOUND WITH THE SURGEON | Annie Claydon |

## July

| | |
|---|---|
| HOW TO FIND A MAN IN FIVE DATES | Tina Beckett |
| BREAKING HER NO-DATING RULE | Amalie Berlin |
| IT HAPPENED ONE NIGHT SHIFT | Amy Andrews |
| TAMED BY HER ARMY DOC'S TOUCH | Lucy Ryder |
| A CHILD TO BIND THEM | Lucy Clark |
| THE BABY THAT CHANGED HER LIFE | Louisa Heaton |